FROM THE GROUND UP

PURPOSED THROUGH PAIN

Melissa A. Melbourne

Fulton Books, Inc.
Meadville, PA

First originally published by Fulton Books 2017

ISBN 978-1-63338-718-8 (Paperback)
ISBN 978-1-63338-574-0 (Digital)

Printed in the United States of America

To my Lord and Savior, thank you for everything. Without you, I would absolutely be nothing. To the best father a girl could have ever asked for, I hope I made you proud. Continue to rest in eternal paradise.

CONTENTS

ACKNOWLEDGEMENTS

To think I'm writing an acknowledgment on a book that I thought would never see the light of day is crazy to me. I've been working on this book for well over three years and every time I began to write I was afraid to tell my truth for fear of being judged. I prayed and asked God to help me be transparent, honest, relatable, and open with this book. The willingness to put myself out there was something I wasn't comfortable with doing, however in an effort to help others I undertook the task of writing this book.

There are so many people I would like to acknowledge with the first being God for giving me the courage and strength to publish a detailed account of my life's journey. In the process of writing this book I've come to realize how therapeutic this was for me. I cried, laughed and was even upset at some of the situations I put myself into. I would like to thank Fulton Book Publishing for seeing this project through in its entirety. I would like to thank my mom and dad for giving me life and for instilling love and kindness in me. I learned a great deal from my parents about character and for that I'm truly humbled to have the best parent's a girl can ever have. To my siblings thank you for being my first set of friends. To all my friends and family there are so many to thank and let's face it if I had to thank everyone personally it would be another book (lol).

I thank you all for your wonderful encouragement and feedback and your constant nagging as to whether or not you all would be in the book. I remembered sending my rough draft to someone that didn't know me and the encouraging feedback that she gave me was the fuel I needed to keep going. I thank you Jinny for being in my corner from the beginning and for believing in me after reading the rough draft of my manuscript. To everyone that I've encountered and have touched my life I thank you for the experience. The idea behind this book was to tell my truth about my life and the experiences that shaped the woman I am today. In no way shape or form did I seek to defame or slander anyone's character in this book.

I thank every one of you all for picking up this book and reading this detailed account of my life's journey. I thank you for believing in me. I couldn't have done this without your love, support, and encouragement.

INTRODUCTION

Friday, October 2, 2015

9:00 p.m.

As I lay here in bed waiting on hurricane Joaquim to pass, I started to think back over my life and instantly began to thank God for my journey, this journey I have been on has not been an easy one per se, its been a rough journey of coming into womanhood, of not asking for permission, but to give the world notice that I have arrived. As I began the process of writing this book I struggled with how it would be received and whether I could be completely transparent with everything that happened in my life. I struggled with the notion of being judged. Could I handle being judged? Am I strong enough to withstand the scrutiny that may come along with this book? Am I ready for what's to come? These were the questions that came to mind while mulling over the idea of putting a detailed account of my life on paper. I went back and forth with God and he decided that judging would have to commence.

My story and experience is not for me, albeit it taught me a great deal about the woman I am today, it's for the man or woman struggling with overcoming adversity or what I like to call life lessons. My story serves to motivate and invoke a spirit of inspiration to those who need it. It is the sole purpose I embarked on this journey of putting my life in the spotlight. I'm finally free from the disease of addiction, I'm now able to show up and be a willing participant in my life. My journey has taught me about forgiveness, patience, strength, persistence, perseverance, resilience, intuitive thinking, and to rely solely on God. So many events have changed the course of my life, but I wouldn't change anything I went through to get through. As I lay here going through old journals, I came across one that specifically chronicled my last rehab attempt. Bad decisions and life lessons had landed me in a treatment facility in the mountains of Waverly, Pennsylvania.

CHAPTER ONE

How Did I Get Here?

March 27, 2007

7:05 p.m.

I arrived at Marworth rehabilitation treatment facility in Waverly Pennsylvania at approximately 7:00 p.m. on March 27, 2007. As the car approached and climbed up this long winding trail of mountainous forest, it somehow reminded me of one those multimillion dollar Beverly Hills mansions. I rolled down the window slightly to get some crisp fresh air in my lungs. The background looked like something you would see on a postcard, it served as the perfect scene out of the movies. It was a sprawling mansion set on about 10 acres of land overlooking ponds, forests, and lakes. As I'm taking in the scenery my mind is racing and my palms began to sweat, am I making the right decision, can I stay clean this time, what's different this time from all the other times. Will I be receptive to treatment or will I continue to pretend that my life hadn't spun out of control? I had hit rock bottom, my disease had progressed to the point where I was suicidal. I was in a volatile, abusive, and tumultuous relationship with a man I used with. I stood at the precipice of life and death. I had taken a semester off from graduate school to keep my demons at bay. I was smoking crack consistently, and school and work was interfering with me getting high (yes I was a functioning addict).

This particular time I was tired of the revolving door, I had been trying to get clean for a long time and couldn't do it on my own successfully. Somehow this time some-thing inside me felt different. I had made up my mind that I wanted to live a healthy lifestyle. I was sick and tired of being sick and tired. I wanted to get and stay clean and I wanted to fix David too. For some strange reason I thought that if I got help, then I could help him and we could live happily ever after. I loved David or at least I thought I did, we had a drug fueled relationship from the very beginning of our relationship, did I really love him or was it the drugs and lifestyle that I loved? I was unsure and couldn't distinguish between the two anymore. One things for certain I knew that this time I wanted and needed help. I had arrived at a place in my life where I was no longer happy with who I was. I was a liar, an addict, a terrible employee, a terrible friend, a disappointment to my parents and a horrible girlfriend. This cycle had been a long continuum from the moment I was introduced to the streets at thirteen years old.

I fell in love with the streets of Perth Amboy, however that love wasn't reciprocated, in fact the streets had chewed me up and spat me out and now I was left to fend for myself, while coping with a nasty crack habit. My disappointment in myself had fueled and exacerbated my drug use, which made me depressed and in return I self medicated to escape my reality. So many questions were racing through my mind such as: how did I get here? What had I become? How did it get this bad? Can I stay clean? What went wrong? Can I live without using drugs for the rest of my life? Why me? As the questions permeated the thoughts in my mind I began to cry. I cried for the woman I longed to become, I cried for the life I lost due to my addiction, I cried for the pain and suffering I put my parents through. I cried mostly because I just wanted to get and stay clean for good.

As the black Lincoln town car approached the front entrance I wiped my tears and gathered myself and my belongings. I was greeted by one of the intake staff who summoned for a staffer to take my belongings to my room. I met with Jessica another intake staff who was full of energy and pleasant. She had me fill out admissions paperwork about myself and my using history. As I'm going through the questionnaire I realize that I was trying my best to minimize my drug use as if my life wasn't out of control already. I quickly stopped and began to answer the questions truthfully. Once I completed the questions I was taken to the medical department where I did all my bloodwork and completed a physical. Afterwards, I was taken to my room and told to relax for the night. I was assigned a buddy who I would meet in the morning; my buddy's role was to help me understand the structure of Marworth as well as engage and foster social interaction with me.

The next day I would awake to a full day of meetings with my assigned counselors and begin my group therapy sessions. I took a shower and retreated to my room for the night. As I laid in my bed in the dark I began crying just thinking about the wreckage of my past. I was a horrible person who hated my very own existence. I knew that this wasn't who I was, but how did I end up like this? How did I become this horrible person? I was in so much emotional pain that I just wanted to escape the pain I was in. Through fighting back tears my mind wrestled with a barrage of emotions. I felt worthless and defeated, my disease had won. I was a crack head who would never amount to anything. My life was a big lie based on my pretentious thinking. As I continued to fight back the many tears that were falling onto the pillow my mind raced back to my childhood as if it was replaying a movie. I thought about everything I had been through up until this very moment. I cried myself to sleep falling into a deep slumber dreaming about my childhood.

Throughout my childhood I was great at pretending. I pretended to be hard when I was really softer than melted ice cream. I hated confrontation, but I couldn't let anyone know that. I pretended like I wasn't smart so I dumbed myself down to fit in and be hard. I was always ready to fight first because I couldn't allow anyone to sense that I feared them. I wanted to be liked and well received by everyone I hung out with so I did whatever they did. I never understood why I pretended so much, I mean I came from a loving and hard working family.

I was raised in a nuclear environment with both my parents and my siblings. My parents worked hard everyday to provide a safe and happy home for their four children. They did the best they could to raise us with the means they had. My parent's were immigrants from Jamaica who migrated to America for a better life for themselves and their children, but some how some where down the line I became detached from my family and became a willing participant in messing up my life with the choices I made. I loved the streets and chose the streets over a traditional upbringing. Who would have thought a skinny likkle maagga gyal from the small island of Jamaica would become an addict at such a young age, thrusted into a world of addiction.

As far as I can remember the odds were against me since birth. I was born on February 15th, 1977 in Victoria

Jubilee Hospital in Kingston, Jamaica. I was born prematurely, one of the only children that gave my mother so much complication during her pregnancy and at birth. She had very high blood pressure that caused her to swell up along with other complications that threatened her chances of carrying me full term. I was born weighing three pounds and 8 ounces to the proud parents of Osbourne and Erlene Melbourne. My dad was super excited because he finally had his baby girl. I was small enough to be held in the palm of my parent's hands, they had to place me on a pillow to hold me. My Parents were told by doctors that I wouldn't survive, not only did I survive I thrived.

My dad had left us when I was very young and came to the United States on a temporary visa; he eventually got his green card while here and began working on bringing his family to America. As a child growing up in Kingston, Jamaica, I was at my happiest, I ate sugar cane, June plum, genapes, chicken back, breadfruit, akee and saltfish, breadfruit, callaloo, curry chicken, oxtails and all the great dishes of my island. In the summers when school was out we would go to the country in Clarendon, Jamaica to visit my dad's family. I would be so excited to be visiting my grandfather, uncles, aunts, and cousins. My grandmother Lena had passed away before I was born so I didn't know her but I heard amazing stories about who she was.

My grandfather Alston Melbourne owned a big farm that housed cows, pigs, chickens, and all sorts of wild animals. His farm was his livelihood so he took pride in his farm. I loved going there because I got to play with all the animals. I remembered vividly an encounter I had with one of the pigs on the farm. One day while on his farm, I was feeding one of my grandpa's pigs and I was being a little bossy. I guess the pig didn't take too kindly to my attitude and bit my pinky finger. My finger split in two and blood gushed everywhere. I ran into the house screaming and crying. My grandpa cleaned me up and kept me inside the house for the day, the next day would you believe it I was back on the farm messing with the same pig that almost took my pinky finger off. As you can see as a young child I loved trouble and was immune to pain and couldn't get enough of it.

I was tiny for my age and loved anything sweet: icicles, ice cream, candy, and everything bad for my health. My favorite candy was called sweetie (A Jamaican candy). I played in big fields, climbed trees, played in bushes, and went to the beaches, national parks, historical gardens and museums. There was always something to do growing up in Jamaica. I remembered my family living at 40 Crescent Road, which was like a big open yard and everyone had their own apartment with a veranda. I lived with my mom and siblings in a tiny one room apartment, we all slept in one bed on top of each other. My brother's Phillip and Oneil were two years apart from each other and were older than me so they never hung out with me, they were too busy playing soccer and netball with each other or hanging with their friends. My sister Audrey was older than all of us so she took care of us when my mom went to town to sell. My sister Audrey was my first best friend I ever had I looked up to her and wanted to be just like her. She was so good to me, she took care of me, played with me, made sure I did my homework and always made sure I was fine, she was like my mom, she cooked, cleaned, and did everything for all of us. I've always admired her strength, grace, resilience and agility. My Brothers Oneil and Phillip on the other hand, were my first heroes they were my big brothers who protected me at all cost. Whenever I had any issues they would be there front and center to protect their baby sister.

As a child they would take me to the store and play with me. They loved me and I loved them. My brothers were very athletic and popular amongst their friends. They played a lot of soccer and netball with their friends in their younger years. They were always active and outside playing. They would play from sun up to sun down. I was a tomboy and always wanted to hangout with them, but they wouldn't allow me to hang out with them. I had friends although their names and faces escape me, I can remember playing with them. I was a happy child always smiling and laughing, however the stories my parents told me about my mom's complicated pregnancy and how she fought tirelessly to get me into this world always made me feel like I was already at a disadvantage. I was the only child she had a lot of complications with, who somehow managed to become the one who gave them the most problems. I always felt different from everyone;

I was always bright and rambunctious yet very shy. I was the poster child for being a good kid growing up. I never got into trouble or gave my parent's any issues. I went to primary school where I wore a blue uniform with a red and white plaid shirt. I loved school and loved to learn and was always a chatterbox. I told everything. Although we were poor, our mom and dad made sure we had the best. My dad would send us money, clothes, shoes and toys from America. My Mom on the other hand was a hustler she would go out hustling by selling things at the market in downtown Kingston. She'd sell whatever she could get her hands on and when she came back home she would cook us dinner, make sure we did our homework, bathe us and get us ready for bed.

On most days when we got out of school we would run down to big yard which was at the bottom of crescent and Spanish town road. My uncle victor (my grandma's brother) owned a big meat store where people came and bought meat and groceries. Everyday uncle victor would go and get his boxes of meat and we would meet him down at big yard to help bring in the boxes of chicken and he would pay us. We would take that money and go buy candy and ice cream or whatever our young hearts desired, the older adults would feed their children with whatever they made helping uncle victor out. Those days were perfect because it not only captured my innocence, but my ability to hustle for whatever I wanted.

My grandmother and aunts were already living in foreign and would come to visit us from Canada. We would be filled with so much excitement because we knew they were coming with goodies for everyone. You see in our young minds we thought foreign was a place where you went and became rich, because every time they came back home to jamaica they had on nice dresses and jewelry and we got so many toys, shoes, and clothes, we couldn't wait to go to foreign. I associated foreign with having nice things. We would get sad when it was time for them to leave. As we approached the airport to drop off my grandma and aunt I would start to get sad because I wanted to know what foreign felt and smelled like. I had never been on a plane and long to know what the inside of a plane looked like. My mom used to tell us one day we will go to foreign, but when would it be our turn?

CHAPTER TWO

New Beginnings

March 12, 1987

The day finally arrived where we would get the chance to come to foreign. I was ten years old when we packed up our things and left Jamaica to come to America. We packed up our things and left Jamaica with the intention of creating the best life possible. My dad had sent for my mom, myself, and my brothers. It was the happiest day of my life I was excited and filled with chatter. My young mind was a playground for my imagination I began to imagine this great life full of riches, big houses and nice clothes. I would finally have my own room and toys to play with. I finally was coming to foreign and I was ecstatic. We left Jamaica with light clothes on. When we arrived at JFK airport in NYC it was freezing cold with the sun peeking behind the cloudy skies. My bones instantly began to shiver and there was white fluffy stuff on the ground that was foreign to me. My dad met us at the airport with coats, hugs, and a huge smile. His huge grin from ear to ear was reminiscent of the pride he felt knowing that he had accomplished what he had set out to do. This was important and an integral role for him as a man. So many Jamaican men left their families behind when they got to America, but my dad didn't do that he worked hard saved his money and brought us here, not only were we proud of him, but his huge smile let us know that he was also proud of himself too. Now back to this white stuff on the ground. I was curious and needed answers as to what this stuff was:

Me: dad what is this white fluffy stuff on the ground

Dad: its snow princess

Me: what's snow?

Dad: fumbling to try his best to explain it, said it's snow on the ground. When it gets cold and cloudy white snowflakes fall out the sky

Me: confused more than ever knew that my dad couldn't really articulate what snow was, I decided to let go of the conversation because I made an instant decision that I didn't like this thing called snow.

I couldn't understand why it was so cold in foreign, this wasn't what my young mind imagined foreign to be. As we rode in silence thinking about how our life had changed in a matter of six hours, I wondered to myself how foreign would treat me, would I like it, would I be able to assimilate quickly, would I make new friends, would they like me, what if they didn't like me, what would school be like, would it be like Jamaica? Would

I adapt? I had so many questions that I silenced the thoughts racing through my mind by slipping into nap.

I awoke to the cab pulling up to 878 Amboy Avenue in Perth Amboy, New Jersey. The house was a blue and white two family house it was a mansion compared to where we were living in Jamaica. It was a 2 bedroom apartment located on the second floor that was kept immaculate with a back yard for us to play in. We were all so happy to finally be in America. We lived across the street from the William Dunlap Homes housing project, which was known as Dunlap. This is where I met my first set of friends Nina and Keisha. They were cool and I loved being around them. I remembered always being at Nina's house or Keisha's house. I loved their grandparents they were always so nice and kind to me. When I wanted to play I would go to Nina's house and ask to play with the girl with the crinkly hair in my heavy Jamaican accent. She had a jheri curl.

Those days were fun we played outdoors from sun up to sundown, hung out at the rec and ate government lunches, we would also hang out down by the factories playing spin the bottle. During the summers we would go to the big baseball field behind Wendy's next to Delaney homes to watch the youth summer baseball leagues. Those times were the best times of my life because I was young and had an air of innocence surrounding me. I enjoyed being a child and loved playing with my new friends. This was right around the beginning of me starting middle school at Samuel e. Shull School, where unknowingly my life would change simply by the crowd I kept.

CHAPTER THREE

Structure

I'm awakened by an intake staff named Connie, who informed me that I'd be meeting with my admissions counselor Mr. James Hart in an hour. She advised me to get dress and head to the dining room to eat breakfast. I got up and proceeded to get dress and eat breakfast. When I met Mr. Hart he was very energetic, attentive, respectful, and knowledgeable about the topic of addiction and recovery. He sounded very promising about the structure of the program and was very prideful on their success rate. They operated at a 90 percent success rate of all their graduates that did the work to stay clean.

They also prided themselves on teaching you the tools to abstain from drugs if we applied it in our daily lives. Although they provided the tools to cope with life without the use of drugs and alcohol, it was imperative that we made meetings and practice the 12 step principles in our lives.

The structure at Marworth was regimented and no nonsense it was similar to boot camp without the sergeants yelling at you. Although this wasn't my first attempt at getting help, something felt different this time around. I was ready to give recovery a shot. I had grown tired of using people, places, and things. I had been living a lie for a long time and this time I was ready to take the mask off. This was the first time that I was excited and optimistic about getting clean. I was excited because I longed for change yet nervous about my future, could I really stay clean was the question I asked myself repeatedly? How would I live without the use of drugs and alcohol? Could I do it? I was nervous because I wasn't sure what came along with that change.

We were up by 6am; breakfast by 7am and group sessions started at 8am and lasted most of the day with NA/AA meetings at night. Our nights ended at 10pm every day. I met so many people that were struggling like me to live a healthy life free from drugs. We all had one goal in mind and that was to stay clean when we got home. I shared about my life up until this point, my disappointment in myself and letting my parents down. For the first time I was purging myself of everything that held me back and brought me to this point in my life.

I was 2 semesters from graduating graduate school at Kean University and a full blown crack addict. I tried to figure out how I had gotten to this point; I mean I had a good job even if I wasn't able to function there anymore. I had a man even though he was someone I was using drugs with for the past 5 years and I had friends who love me and wanted to see me well. Naturally I felt like I was doing a lot better than most I just needed to get a handle on things and even though I tried to keep up the façade that I was doing well for myself my life was falling apart right in front of my eyes. I no longer knew who I was anymore.

I was broken and suicidal and had no reason to live or so I thought. I had been wearing multiple masks and losing myself deeper and deeper the more I used. I hated who I had become the drugs had eaten me alive. I was less than 98lbs by the time I entered Marworth. I looked like a crack head. I was gaunt and sickly and my cheeks were sunken in. I had gotten to a point where I was sick and tired of using drugs but didn't know how to stop. I had an obsession and compulsion with using drugs. My life was centered on my addiction. No longer was I interested in school or work. I had become isolated from everyone; it would be months before anyone of my immediate friends or family member would hear form me. It was just me and David and we enabled each other.

The sad thing is we were both hurting and couldn't help each other. We both knew that we deserved better and wanted more but we were in the grips of the disease of addiction.

The few weeks I was in treatment at Marworth I learned a lot about my disease through intensive therapy sessions. I learned the disease of addiction is a morally deficient disease that is centered in your thinking. I also learned that the disease is cunning, baffling, and insidious. Knowing what I learned through those group sessions I knew I could never be complacent with this disease. I began to take inventory over my life and what I started to realize was that I loved being in the mix of everything and I used behind my feelings. I was always people pleasing from a little girl, I also hated confrontation, and being picked on. From the first day I met a group of friends I realized that I followed their lead and did whatever I could to fit in. I remembered meeting these friends in middle school while on the girl's basketball team at Samuel E. Shull School. Even though they had a little structure at home they did whatever they wanted and I was envious of that. They were raised by single parents or their grandparents and could do whatever they wanted, me on the other hand I had to ask for permission and the answer was always NO my parents were very protective and overbearing.

The more I hung out and socialized with my friends the more I resented my parents for being so protective. I mean these girls were independent and did whatever they wanted. I was jealous because I wished I could do whatever I wanted. I wasn't allowed to do anything but go to school and come home after school. I hung out with these girls during school and at the after school program. Sometimes I would sneak and hangout with them after school on days when my parents worked late. I was able to sneak and hangout with them because my parents worked crazy hours and a lot of overtime. Oftentimes I would be alone for long periods of time, so I started sneaking outside when my brothers were gone or hanging out with their friends. The more I hung out with them the more I wanted to hang out in the streets. I snuck around hanging out with them for about two years until I began high school.

CHAPTER FOUR

Rebel Without a Cause

I didn't really start drinking and smoking until I got to high school. I liked my friends a lot because they didn't judge me or crack on me. During middle school I was always being cracked on for being too dark skinned, too skinny, too black, and too ugly. I was called everything from black crow to blacky to pencil legs you name it. My classmates were ruthless in their verbal and physical attacks against me. I started getting into fights and getting suspended and rebelling while in middle school. I quickly became known as bad and I was okay with that label even if I didn't understand the negative connotation that came along with being labeled bad. I didn't care about the label, I wouldn't allow anyone to punk me; part of my defense mechanism was to fight anyone who disrespected me and that's what I did. With my friends they didn't treat me like that and I wanted to prove to them that I was down and loyal in order to be apart of the clique. In a short period of time things started to change. I was hanging out past my curfew I started not coming home after school. I began to lie to my parents about everything. My attitude slowly began to change;

I was a freshman in high school now. I had learned so much from hanging out after school with my friends that I became enamored with the streets. I was learning the ropes and having fun, this was the life (so I thought). I began disrespecting my parents and being belligerent in school. Within a year of being in high school I had done a 360. My parents no longer knew who their child was. They tried beating me, getting me counseling, hell even some form of voodoo, none of it worked. I was gone.

In an effort to be as truthful as possible I feel the need to elucidate a little bit more about my high school experience which wasn't as bad as I would like to think it was. I met some of my best friends in high school, both of whom are my best friends until today. I met Magreta and Diana in my algebra 1a class they both thought I was funny and crazy I made them laugh every time I came to class after being gone for long periods. Magreta was quiet, kind and chill she was always supportive in helping me with my homework and anything I needed her help with. We grew close from the moment we met.

Diana was also very quiet, observant and reserved; she too thought I was crazy and funny. She could always count on me to make her laugh and that I did. We became close once we knew that we had the same circle of friends and family as I'd like to call them. From that moment forward we clicked and hung out whenever I came to class and outside of school. Diana and Magreta are still one of my closest friends that I can call and talk to about anything.

On days when I came to school I was always begging the teacher to go back weeks to catch me up to speed on what lessons I had missed. As I've mentioned before I was very smart and was able to pick up where I left off whenever I came to class, but I was also a comedian who never took anything serious enough when it came to school. Every time I resurfaced I expected the teacher to catch me up to speed on lessons I missed, she would smile and be so patient with me and help me to catch up either after class or after school.

My math teacher Mrs. Silberberg was heaven sent I loved her and she loved me. She believed in me from the day I walked into her class. She exhibited true patience when it came to working with me one on one. From the first day I entered her classroom she saw a beautiful, assertive, smart, articulate, comedic, and eager to learn young girl. She would speak so much positivity to me that she made me believe in myself and want to do better for myself against all the bad things I was doing with my life, she was the first person to believe in me and pour into my potential. She was the first person to plant a seed within me and make me believe that I could actually become someone. She would tell me the world was my oyster if I just believed in myself. I had no clue what that meant at the time, but this tiny woman saw something in me that I couldn't see in myself. I know that she would beam with pride to see how well my life turned out.

Mrs. Silberberg was a tiny woman no more than 5'4" very slim with dark olive skin reminiscent of her Italian Sicilian ancestors, she had curly hair and always looked polished. She took pride in her appearance and always looked her best. She had a quiet strength to her, rarely did you see her upset her spirit was kind, loving, caring and welcoming. She later became my guidance coun-selor and that's when I really got to know her. I was in the 10th grade at the time, every time I would go to her office to see her I always made her laugh and She would always tell me how beautiful I am and that I could be anything I wanted to be, but I never believed her because my environment told me otherwise. I simply couldn't see myself being anything more than an alcoholic drunk. My love for the streets outweighed my love for myself; my life revolved around the streets and school was secondary to that. I honestly believed that I would die in those streets. I didn't have any ambition or drive I just wanted to party all the time and that's what I did.

The streets had gotten a hold of me and I welcomed it with open arms. By this time I was at least 16 if my memory serves me correctly. I was drinking like a fish and took a liking to it. I didn't get regular drunk like normal people I got drunk and passed out, peed on myself, and fought people. I quickly became the crazy drunk Jamaican girl, who got drunk and did crazy things. The Perth Amboy police department knew me on a first name basis. I was always getting locked up for a myriad of things like being drunk, disorderly conduct, fighting, shoplifting and fighting the cops. I would get black out drunk and be so embarrassed about what I did in a drunken state that I would drink as soon as I got up to escape whatever stories were told to me about me. I quickly became the town drunk, I was written off as a drunk and would be nothing in life, even my parents believed that I wouldn't amount to anything. (Their words exactly).

I loved alcohol that was my drug of choice. As I started getting older I began to experiment with harder drugs. I began smoking woolies (it's a mixture of crack cocaine and weed} and coolies {a mixture of crack cocaine and cigarettes). I fell in love because it did two things it made me high as hell and slowed me down when I drank. I was in heaven. As my drinking exacerbated the more I used drugs. I now could get drunk as hell and smoke woolie blunts and feel like I'm on top of the world. I had no cares in the world and continued in this vicious cycle for as long as I could. The more I used the higher my tolerance became.

My teenage years, which was suppose to be my formative years were spent in a haze of weed smoking, drinking, taking acid trips, smoking woolie blunts and selling drugs. School was no longer an option. I was hustling coke, smoking woolie blunts and wasting away. I had no ambition even though from time to time I thought about what Mrs. Silberberg used to tell me. I quickly dismissed those thoughts and hit the block running. I spent those years getting in and out of trouble for disorderly conduct, drunk and lewd conduct, shoplifting, fighting, and a felony drug charge for possession of narcotics (cocaine) with intent to distribute. Ill get more into that shortly.

Even while I was wasting away in the streets my dad still wouldn't give up on me, He was determined to not let the streets take his daughter. He used to come around the Huntington building in his big red truck looking for me and I would be hiding behind the garbage can or in the building. He would threaten everyone he came in contact with regarding my whereabouts. He hated who I had become and felt the only way to save me was by beating me, embarrassing me, or coming to snatch me up to take me home. It didn't change anything I still did what I wanted when I wanted.

For some strange reason I thought my childhood was typical, aside from my dad chasing me around town looking to save me by any means necessary. I knew he loved me and did those things because he wanted the best for me. He knew I was a smart kid who was making some terrible choices. He tried his best to save me from the streets, but I wasn't interested in walking a straight path. I wanted to be in the streets that was the choice I made. My parents worked hard to provide for us; however, I think the stress I put on my parents quickly began to pull them in different directions. My mom was quiet and didn't talk much. She kept her feelings to herself and wouldn't speak to me much, my dad on the other hand was loud and boisterous, always looking for me to beat me up, embarrass me, yell at me or drag me home. The toll it took on my parents lead them to fight often about everything under the sun.

My earlier memories of my father weren't always the fondest memories I'd like to remember of him. My dad was a very hardworking functioning alcoholic; he never missed a day of work no matter the weather or if he was under the weather. His work ethic was incomparable. He was a great provider and lovable man that I loved immensely when he wasn't drinking, which became nonexistent at one point in our lives. I honestly believe this is how he coped with the stressors of life.

For a while he was always mad about everything. Some days when he was in a great mood, we would be a happy family, but there were days when he was nasty when he drank. On days when he was happy he would be in the living room playing all the great Jamaican classics like Peter tosh, Dennis brown, yellow man, garnet silk, beres Hammond and so much more on his dj set dancing, drinking his budweiser and smoking a spliff. We would dance and have a great time, but other times he was a nasty drunk (This is where I got it from when I drank). He would curse and argue and call us names. I knew my dad loved me, however when he drank he sent mixed signals because he would curse me out and call me a whore, ugly, and tell me things like I'm worthless, and that I would never amount to anything.

As a child of 11-12 that impacted my thinking, because I began to internalize those things and think to myself if that's what he sees, then I'm sure that's what everyone else sees and that's what I am. I was always teased in school for being black, skinny, and ugly. I created this self defense mechanism where I made fun of myself before anyone else would make fun of me. I figured if I highlighted my flaws no one else could use them against me. It was my way of being in control of how you viewed me. I wanted people to view me as funny. What this behavior did was make me super critical of myself (until this day). I never felt like I was good enough I was always joking about how black and ugly I was in an effort to get people to laugh with me instead of at me. So not only was I fighting off the views of my peers at a young age. I was fighting against the thoughts of my own parent and figuring out a defense mechanism to counter the barrage of attacks that were coming against me from my peers. That fucked me up for a long time because I was always talking negatively about myself to myself. Pessimism and self doubt were always at the forefront of my thinking.

CHAPTER FIVE

Mirrored Effect

My father's alcoholism shaped how I felt about myself and how I viewed men. I associated love with verbal abuse and that's how my selection process in men began. I can remember being in the streets drunk and high and going to parties. None of the guys would hook up with me until they were shitfaced drunk then they would talk to me. I was the last of their selection. I was the girl that guys denied hooking up with. I was the last choice always. I was never good enough for anyone. Somehow my father's hateful words all stayed with me (you're worthless, ugly, and won't amount to nothing). I began to believe that I wasn't worth shit and would never amount to anything. I became a drunken, promiscuous, belligerent, and self destructive young girl. I was a blackout drunk who peed all over myself whenever I drank, which was daily. I hated myself and was looking for a way to kill myself. Drugs were my only escape from these horrible feelings I felt. Many times I drank to die and every day that I woke up I cursed God. I wanted to be loved by my father and be told that I was beautiful, but those things were far and few when he drank. I wanted to be normal. I always felt like I stuck out like a sore thumb and could never quite fit in. I suffered silently for many years with being depressed and as a result the drinking and drug use got worse.

Through extensive therapy I learned my father was an alcoholic and didn't mean the things he said when he drank. I rebelled as a cry for help because I didn't see my worth or developed any self confidence during my adolescent years. I didn't believe anything anyone told me about my potential. I was homeless and living with people because of the choices I was making. I can remember a few people I lived with while living on the streets. One of them was my friend Mesha.

I met Mesha in the streets we were cool we used to chill and smoke blunts together. I used to hang out at her house with her and her abuela Maria so much that I just started living with them. I loved her abuela she was a firecracker and full of energy. She was funny, charismatic, and very loving. She stood about five feet with deep dark chocolate brown skin tone, her skin was smooth like silk and she had short pretty curly hair. She reminded me of the Oshun Goddess. She was small up top with a small waist and a derriere that stopped every-one in their tracks; she was the backbone of the family. Her Puerto Rican heritage was infused in every dish she made. I loved her cooking and how structured she kept her home. She loved me like I was one of her own. I had chores like everyone else. She never bothered me and I was always respectful to her and her household.

I lived with Mesha and her Abuela for about a year or so. Mesha and I grew closer than before once I moved in with them. We did everything together we ran the streets and did our dirt together. We would get drunk and smoke blunts together as I mentioned before. She was a beautiful chubby Puerto Rican girl with beautiful olive skin and beautiful long black hair synonymous to Pocahontas. She was and still is beautiful. We had a lot of fun hanging out with each other. I moved around so much that before I knew it I was living somewhere else. I'm grateful to Mesha and her grandmother for treating me like family and taking me in when I had no place to go.

My parents had given up on me and wanted nothing to do with me and I wanted nothing to do with them. I started making choices that weren't conducive to what I wanted out of life. I was looking for love from anyone and anything. My first taste of mistreatment came by way of what I thought was someone who liked me, who just happened to be someone I lost my virginity to. I figured he liked me because he showed me some form of attention. We met at a party and exchanged pager numbers and began seeing each other shortly after, he drove so he would come and get me, one weekend I went to his house in another town and I had sex with him. It was the most painful thing I ever experienced and I knew instantly that I wouldn't be doing this again any time soon. I started to fall for him and as you guessed it he dissed me a few weeks later. A couple of weeks later I felt something wasn't right down there so I went to planned parenthood and true to my intuition he had given me crabs. I was angry, hurt, confused, yet thankful it wasn't something worst. It took me about a year and a half to even think about having sex or talking to anyone. I was hurt because this guy had to have known he had crabs and knowingly sleeping with women and passing it on.

About a year and a half later I hooked up with a slightly older guy at a basement party who happened to be a popular drug dealer in our town. I fell head over heels for him because everybody knew him and he commanded respect everywhere he went. I really liked this guy, but he made it clear I wasn't good enough for him by his actions. He was a womanizer with a stable of women and I eagerly accepted the role as a side chick. He only called me up late in the night and I would come running no matter where I was. He never kissed me or made me feel loved. He just used to get on top of me and stick it in get his pleasure and that was it.

In my mind I knew that wasn't what I wanted but I had convinced myself that this guy liked me regardless of what his actions said. He would see me in the streets and wouldn't even speak to me and when he did it was usually in a conversation setting where he would be talking to someone else and slightly acknowledge my existence. I was so shy and scared to tell anyone including him how I felt. I didn't like being used for sex but I didn't know how to say no so I became ok with it because

I was happy someone wanted me even if it was 3am in the morning. He would sleep with me and wake me up before the sun came up to tell me to leave. I would have to find my way home. He never offered a cab fare or a ride. I hated myself and allowed this guy to mistreat me because I thought I wasn't worth anything and I didn't know how to say NO. I told myself I wasn't worthy of any love, look how I looked I was tall, goofy, awkward, and ugly. I was constantly used for sex by this guy and treated like garbage that I honestly believed that was how you treated a woman. That was how I picked these guys based on how badly they could/would treat me. I felt like if they treated me that way they really liked me. I drank and drugged to escape the incessant thoughts of feeling worthless.

CHAPTER SIX

Streets Are Watching

I never really quite fit in with the smart kids, nor the athletes, nor the pretty or popular girls I always felt like a misfit no matter how hard I tried; I gave up trying and didn't care to fit in any longer. The only people I found myself fitting in with were misfits and people from the block so that's who I gravitated to. I was tired of people treating me however they wanted to and although I kept people pleasing I just said fuck it and started hanging out with people who wanted to be around me. That solved the problem real quick. In high school I was loud, obnoxious, ratchet and gossiped about everyone, plus I was always cracking jokes on people. People thought I was funny as hell but I was just making them laugh long enough not to focus on me. I hated when people acted like I wasn't good enough to be around them. I didn't have those issues with my friends, because I had found a new sense of family with my best friends Kenja and Nisha. Like I mentioned earlier I met both of them in Middle school when we were on the girls' basketball team at Samuel E. Shull School, we clicked instantly and became close. Nisha was a star athlete, Kenja was good, and I was the crazy wild trouble maker who was always fighting on and off the court.

The love of basketball brought us together. We would chill at nisha's house after school and eat cheesesteak and fries sandwiches and watch video music box, we would be so excited to see the new hip hop videos that came out. Nisha was always rapping and writing raps and I was the hype man. Those days were the good ole fun days where we looked forward to the programs they had at the recreation center in the building (that's what we called the Huntington building) we would play cards, ping pong or always go on trips, I loved those days because we were inseparable and her family loved me like I was their own family. At the building everyone was a close knit family that took care and looked out for each other no matter what. We were a family and we acted in that manner. We protected each other from outsiders at all cost.

I remembered one summer afternoon in the mid 1990's we had a huge fight with some girls from old bridge. I'm sure I started it as I started all the fights when I was drunk. People would always want to fight me because I was a trouble maker and they assumed because I was tall and skinny that I couldn't fight, they were quickly reminded that their assumption wasn't always right. I was quick with my hands and loved to fight. Unbeknownst to them, I really didn't care whether I won, lost or it was a draw, I was crazy and loved a good fight. Back to this particular day, it was an all out brawl in the streets of Hall Ave and Cortlandt St, it was no more than four or five of us and it was an army of girls. We beat them up something terribly. People came from all over to help us beat up those girls, it was surreal and something that you would see in a movie. The familial bond that everyone had at the building wouldn't allow for anyone to interfere with us or them so we stuck together and fought battles together. Everyone knew each other and wouldn't let anything happen to each other and that's what I loved about the Huntington building. Our sisterly bond with each other grew stronger over time as we explored everything together.

Nisha was the ring leader who had very good leadership qualities about her if channeled correctly. We followed her lead even though she wasn't bossy. She had seen a lot growing up so she learned quickly how to navigate through life. She didn't tell her business and she wasn't quick to meet new people, she was reserved and observant yet very diplomatic with everyone that came into contact with her. She was chocolate and stocky with a gorgeous smile and thick course beautiful black hair her skin was pure chocolate cocoa. She stood about 5'7" with tom boyish qualities. She was very well respected from a very young age; she observed everything and when she spoke she usually made a lot of sense for her age. She was cool and got along with everyone. She had a kind and caring spirit about her.

We became inseparable from the moment we met on the basketball court in middle school. She had a big family who all lived in the same house with her. Her uncle aunts and cousins all lived with her and her grandmother. I was close to Nisha and absorbed everything she did. We earned each other's trust and I was able to learn a lot about street life together, of course I was fascinated with this life because I was rebelling against my own traditional upbringing. We drank and got high together and did our dirty work together.

Kenja was my party buddy who loved to have a good time and laugh. She was always down for whatever. We connected because of our kindred spirits to each other. She is funny and a fighter just like me. She was pretty tall like me and slightly lighter than me, we were often times mistaken for sisters. Everything about Kenja was cool and fun. We liked to drink and have a good time and that's what we did. We would drink and I would start trouble and her and Nisha would be there to fight with me and we would laugh about it. The mid 90's was a time of exploration for all of us. We were young and curious and attracted to the street life so that peeked our interest.

We did a lot of exploration and experimenting, but always went back to our drug of choice which for me was drinking. We all got along because we didn't judge each other. We spoke our minds and left nothing off limits. I believe it was that openness and willingness to make our friendship work that kept us together for as long as it did. Life has a way of pulling everyone in different directions, we all suffered similar fates with addiction but thanks to God we are still in the land of the living. Kenja and I are still very good friends. Nisha and I speak but we don't see each other as often as I'd like to. I have a lot of love and respect for those ladies we went through a lot of things together.

Nisha's grandmother's name was Mattie Joe, Mattie Joe was a no nonsense woman with a heart of gold who could cook anyone under the table. She stood less than five feet tall and was round and stout with a smile that warmed up any room. She wore strength like it was clothing and had a heart of gold, she was and still is funny and loving even when she was fussing me out. She was a woman of God that introduced me to church at an early age. I remembered we used to be in church acting up and all it took was one look to straighten us up. She treated me like her own blood and loved me. She loved all her children and grandchildren good bad or indifferent. She had already raised all her children and was now raising her grandchildren. I slept in nisha's room and had chores like the rest of the kids. Every now and then she would kick me out when I came home drunk and acting crazy and I would be right back there the next day. I loved Mattie Joe and my extended family. She treated one no different than the other. This was my home if anyone was looking for me I was always at Mattie Joe's house in apt 3f at the Huntington building. That's where I was raised if you asked me. They loved me and I loved them and as far as I was concerned they are my family up until today.

I learned a lot about the operations and profit of drugs from an economical stand point from hanging around the building. I knew who hustled, who got high, who the johns were, what time the money rolled in, how to cook, bag up, and sell coke. I learned how to operate the streets of Hall Ave, Cortland St, the tracks behind the high school, and the back streets surrounding the Huntington building. That's were we did our dirt. When I wanted to hide out and smoke a woolie blunt I would hide out on the tracks behind the building. Summers were always fun at the building because everyone came on our side of town to hang out. Hall ave was a prime hangout spot in the mid 1990's. We would hang out on crates in front of the Chinese store and Ms. Judy's bar and hustle. We would buy all of our liquor from Ms. Judy's bar where she had the coldest forty ounces in history. We would be outside drinking St. Ides, southern comfort, mad dog, cisco, wild irish rose and listening to the latest rap music, getting drunk and breaking night in the back of the building near the basketball court.

The first time I experienced a drunken black out episode was in the back of the building. It was a regular day and I had been drinking all day without incident and then the next minute all I could remember was feeling like someone was doing an exorcism on me. I don't remember all the details except what was told to me. Apparently I was blacked out drunk and acting crazy rolling on the ground and hitting my head on the wall and throwing up everywhere. When they tried to pick me up to walk I couldn't walk. My legs would collapse at every attempt I made to walk it was an embarrassing moment one that I quickly pushed in the back of my mind because I didn't want to come to terms with the fact that I could quite possibly be a black out alcoholic at such a young age. I pushed that episode in the back of my head as if it never happened and continued to party.

There was always a party going on somewhere in the building. I remembered junior used to always have parties either in the rec or in his house on the 6th floor. Those parties were fun papo would dj and we would be in a state of nostalgia as the hip hop beats penetrated our bodies and the weed smoke permeated the air. Junior threw the best house parties ever that attracted party goers from all over the city. These were the sweet memories I had of the Huntington building. It was memories of love, fun, family, tragedy, but more importantly a sense of community. These memories helped to shape the woman I am today. The building taught me about family, loyalty, and respect. By late 1990's developers were moving in on prime real estate in the city of Perth Amboy. The projects were being torn down for the purpose of gentrification. I believe they wanted the city of Perth Amboy to become more appealing to real estate developers, in an effort to attract a different group of people. They had pushed everyone out of the building and moved people to various parts of the city. Aunt Mattie Joe moved to the Stockton building and I was right there with her.

CHAPTER SEVEN

Bad to Worse

Once we moved to the Stockton building things got progressively worse for me, my disease was progressing at an alarming rate. The only good thing about the Stockton building was that we had access to the downtown smith street area and that's where we did most of our hanging out (code for hustling). I hustled in bars like cowboy johns, b&b's, booger hut, on the streets and a few of the Mexican bars on Smith St. Smith St was party central for us, which was where everything was happening in the late 90's. This is exactly where I caught my first and only felony. (More on that later) I was wild by this time in my life. I was smoking woolies in Philly blunts and still drinking more than ever. I was what was known as a woo head. That's all I liked to do was smoke woolies get drunk and sells drugs. I had a Spanish boyfriend at the time that was a pipe head; he never did any of it around me. He just used to fuck up my product a lot and lie about it until I found out he smoked coke then I was done with him. I wasn't exposed to the pipe yet nor was I interested. I was still smoking woolie blunts heavily, oftentimes fucking up my own packages. I was smoking heavily and couldn't keep up with my own packages so now I had to hustle for other people in order to get a cut. I would do that long enough until I got my money up to buy own grams of coke to get back on. This was how I maintained my habit.

I was going a hundred miles an hour. Nisha had moved on Meade Street and I was living there with her and her son my god son Amir. We partied all day into the night, at this point heroin is now being introduced into our partying. I tried it a few times out of fun and decided that wasn't my thing. I didn't like anything that made me nod and scratch. I liked coke and if I could have done it without any consequences I would, but that wasn't the case. I was running wild until one fateful night it all caught up to me.

March 11, 1996

I was drunk as usual nothing was out of the ordinary, I was up drinking and drugging all night and continued into the day and throughout the night. By midnight I was literally fucked up, from what was told to me. We were in front of the Jamaican restaurant on Smith St loitering and someone called the cops. The cops came and apparently I told them to get the fuck outta here I'm tryna sell my drugs or some shit like that. I was arrested on the spot and put in the back of the police car, while I was in the police car I was trying to get the cocaine out of my panties and couldn't, when they brought me to the police station they knew I was obviously drunk they took their time processing me for disorderly conduct. Once they finally processed me they allowed me to use the bathroom. I used the bathroom and tried to flush the package down the toilet not realizing that the toilet didn't have any water in it to flush the drugs. They found the drugs after I used the bathroom. I tried to deny it, but my criminal record had superseded me. I was charged with possession of a controlled dangerous substance with intent to distribute within a school zone. I was transported to the Middlesex County Adult corrections Center.

I woke up the next morning in the county jail scared and not knowing what happened. I called my parents and they couldn't believe what had happened to me, they were yelling at me over the phone telling me that I ruined my life. I knew that they were disappointed in me just by the tone in my father's voice. I sat in jail for four days before I made bail; my parents had put their house up for collateral and bailed me out. The ride from the county to my parents' house felt like we were traveling down south. It was filled with silence for the first five minutes then my dad yelled and screamed about what he wouldn't tolerate anymore and that he didn't bring me to America to ruin my life. At the rate I was going I was sure going to ruin my life. I didn't want to here any of what my dad was saying, in my head I was thinking about getting drunk and high. I left the same night I got home to my parents house, they were living in Avenel, NJ at this time. I had to walk at least a mile to the bus stop but on this particular night I was happy to walk that mile because I knew in a short bus ride I would be in Amboy reconnected with my friends and getting drunk.

I chilled out selling drugs for a little or rather I got smart. I started holding the coke in my mouth so I can swallow them quickly. I quickly picked up where I left off. In that process nothing had changed I was still doing the same thing day in and day out, but now I started dabbling in heroin to get the edge off me when I got too high.

I didn't like the way heroin made me feel because I hated being down, I liked the speed of coke, but the heroin equalized the synergistic effects of both drugs together. I was smoking coke now more than ever and chasing the high with heroin. I began to get that monkey on my back feeling where I would need a bag of heroin in the morning in order for me to function. I quickly stopped using heroin because I knew if I didn't stop I could quite possibly overdose. In the midst of my drug use I'm going back and forth to court trying to get a plea deal to get my case lowered to a program rather than jail time, but because I already had a juvenile record the judge took that into account and I was offered a plea deal. I copped out to the plea deal of 237 days in county jail and 4 years probation. I was scheduled to appear in court on December 3rd, 1996 to begin my sentence.

CHAPTER EIGHT

Divine Intervention

On December 3rd 1996 I reported to the Middlesex County Superior Court for my sentence and was arrested and placed in the custody of the Middlesex County Adult Corrections Center. Upon arrival I was taken to the medical unit. There they drew my bloodwork and tested me for any possible diseases or std's before placing me into population. I was in the medical unit for at least three or four days before being placed into population. I was given an orange jumpsuit at first and once I got through my medical evaluation and put into population I was given one pair of green khaki's and a green corrections tee shirt anything else I had to fend for myself. When I walked into the female unit it was a big open space that had the correction officer's station at the front and as you continue to walk into the back of the unit it was open tables with plastic chairs and two tiers that were filled with cells. The open space housed one small TV for our viewing pleasure. To the side of the open space was a small room that we would go to if we wanted to go to church or NA meetings whenever they came. It was a noisy unit from the sounds of chatters and the doors being buzzed opened and closed

As I searched the room I saw some familiar faces from the streets that I knew from either selling them drugs or getting high with them so I felt a little comfortable yet still scared. I was locked in a cell after breakfast, lunch, and dinner. I was told when to eat, sleep, and shit. I hated the food and cried everyday. The water was hard and left my skin ashy after every shower. I absolutely abhorred this place, but this was my home. I had a new roommate every week, and they were always kicking dope and throwing up and shitting on themselves. In place of cigarettes they would smoke dried up lettuce in paper. I remembered my first and only fight I had with this inmate named Kim. I don't recall what her issues with me were all I know I was on the phone with my dad talking about our usual upcoming visits on Sundays and she came up to me and told me to get the fuck off the phone. At first I looked around wondering who she was talking to so I ignored her and kept talking to my dad and then she started talking shit about how she wanted to use the phone and I was over my time. She hung up the phone while I was in mid sentence talking to my dad. I swear on everything I loved I beat the shit out that girl. I had so much anger and rage in me the correction officer's thought I was going to kill her. After I was pulled off of her they shut the entire unit down and I was locked up in solitary for a few days. I lost my mind in that cell it was in that very moment I began praying asking god for another chance at life. Three days later I was released from solitary confinement and for the rest of my sentence I was respected by everyone. I was known as the crazy Jamaican girl. I laid low got a job in the kitchen went to the law library and church.

My time being incarcerated was a time where a lot of things were revealed to me and I saw things a lot more clearly. My friends were non existent, no one wrote me except for my best friend Jennifer. She and her mom came to visit me aside from my dad who visited me faithfully every Sunday. He would cry to the guards to let me out, not really understanding that I was sentenced and couldn't be released until I served my time. My mom on the other hand wasn't that keen on seeing her daughter in jail so she never visited me. My time away from home made me realize how precious my freedom was, I promised myself I wouldn't come back, and spoke highly of what I would do when I got home. I met some great people and some not so great people while incarcerated. I saw so many women who were institutionalized by the system. It was a revolving door for them coming in and going out. I can remember speaking with some of the guards who would encourage me to not get caught up in the system. They would tell me I was beautiful, articulate, and smart and this was no place for me, of course I didn't believe what they were saying. I was conditioned to think that I was absolutely nothing and would become nothing, but I played along and talked a good game. I was liked by everyone in jail, I learned the ropes and got along with everyone because I was a jokester and that's what got me through. I stayed in my lane and was very diplomatic with everyone and never had an issue aside from the fight I had with kim who unbeknownst to me was mentally challenged. I guess you could say I was chameleon.

Some days I longed to go home and eat a good home cooked Jamaican meal. I had a lot of time to read, watch TV, and study the bible. I thought about my life up until this point, I knew I was smart, I was told that all my life, but I didn't believe it because I had developed this warped sense of self. I suffered from low self esteem, no confidence, displaced anger and lack of self aware-ness, which lead to my drug use. I never thought I was good enough for anyone or anything including myself. I always met the bottom of the barrel guys that treated me like shit, so as a result I was attracted to dudes that treated me like shit. I was never good enough to be seen in public with them or be in a public relationship with them. I was a jump off and booty call when they got drunk and high, and I would easily oblige as long as they kept the party going.

A lot of that had to do with my relationship with my father. I knew he loved me, there was enough palpable evidence to prove his love for me, I loved my dad so I didn't hold that against him because I became just like him. When I got drunk I was sad, mad, angry, and said mean things to people that would cause me to get into fights. I was young, rebellious, and acting out which all caught up to me. Here I am lying on a cot in a jail cell celebrating my 20th birthday and thinking over my life. I vowed that I would never be put in another position as this one. I knew I wanted better, but I didn't believe in myself enough to know how I would do better. I was safe in jail and so were my thoughts. I had big dreams once I got out. I would go back to school and go on to become someone. From a kid I used to daydream that when I grew up my name would somehow be in lights. I was determined to see my name in lights when I got out.

I laid on my cot during one of the many breaks we had in jail and fell into a slumber where I dreamt about being a supermodel and traveling all over the world with Naomi Campbell, Cindy Crawford and all the top notch models modeling for different designers wearing the latest and the best in designer labels, as my dream came to a close I was transported back to reality by the sound of the buzzer for us to come back out of our cell for dinner.

I awoke and in that moment knew I would never come back to this place. At that moment I made the decision I wanted the best life had to offer and I was going to do just that, I didn't know how I was going to do it but I vowed to do it. Looking back over my life with a different set of eyes I now know that this was God's divine plan and intervention for my life. I was going 100 miles an hour and headed for death, I now know that I needed to sit still because it was apparent my life was going downhill very fast.

CHAPTER NINE

A Second Chance

May 27, 1997 I was scheduled to be released from jail. I didn't sleep all night thinking about everything I planned on doing. I had a laundry list of things I wanted to do in one day. I wanted to go to the beach, the mall, hair salon and nail shop. That morning I awoke jittery, nervous, and scared, all those talks I had been having with God were now becoming my reality. Would I let God, myself, or my family down? Would I rise above adversity? Or would these revolving doors be my new reality? Those were the questions that weighed heavy on my mind on the morning I awoke. I got up did my hair, got dressed, and walked up to guard station. I said my good byes to the guards who were happy to see me go and start my new life. From there I was transported to the front entrance where I did my exit paper work and was released. The day was bright and sunny and warm. The sun kissed my face in small strokes causing me to smile. The air was crisp and smelled like freedom. My dad awaited me in his shiny white kia optima. I got in and we talked on the way home, mostly him about me changing my life and getting myself together, I just listened and thanked God for my freedom. I got home and enjoyed the comfort of a warm Jamaican dish, my bed and my family. The next few days I just stayed home and relaxed and strategized.

After a week or so I followed up with my probation officer. Her name was Karen she was young, vibrant, talkative, and straightforward in her delivery. She meant business and was seasoned in how she operated. She went over what was expected of me in order to complete probation and avoid returning to jail, she told me I would be randomly drug tested so I need to keep my nose clean and I would be fine. With her there weren't any second chances and I was determined not to go back to jail. I was given strict orders from Karen, those orders were to go back to school and get a job immediately so I can pay back my fines. The next day I went down to the Perth Amboy Adult School and signed up for school, I also went and applied for a job at ShopRite. I began going to the adult school and working at ShopRite, things were going great for a few months as I assimilated back into society. I was happy I had a job and back in school even if I went when I felt like it. Although things were starting to fall into place, I found myself slowly falling back into old patterns and habits. I was hanging with the same old crew and drinking more than ever, because of my random drug testing I stayed away from the hard drugs. I was to determine not to go back to jail.

School was going great whenever I showed up, I remembered my counselor at the adult school Mr. Shelton telling me how smart I was and how he can see me going to college. I told him college isn't for me. He told me in no uncertain terms if I don't go to college I would be going back to jail and I instantly became scared because I didn't want to go back to jail. So I began to listen. He told me that he sees so much potential in me. You are too smart for adult school don't waste your life is what he told me; He also told me that I needed to come to school more often in order to graduate. That conversation reso- nated with me because for once I believed him.

I knew I wanted better for my life hell I deserved better. I decided to give school a shot and started going more frequently and passing my courses, before I knew it I completed adult school and got my high school diploma. I was happy, but wanted more. Mr Shelton had planted a seed in me and I wanted to test the waters of college. I told myself I would go for one semester and if I didn't like it I would drop out so I decided to give myself a shot and signed up for Middlesex County College.

I started Middlesex County College the fall semester September of 1999; I was scared and excited because I couldn't believe I was actually in college. It was a whole new experience for me. I didn't know what I was doing, what would be my major? What do I want to do with my life? I had no clue but I figured I had to start somewhere. I was intimidated, anxious, yet proud of myself and the strides I was making to better myself and prove everyone wrong especially my father who told me I wouldn't amount to shit.

My first semester consisted of all remedial courses. I wasn't surprised that I picked up where I had left off in high school. I began plugging away, absorbing and processing information as well as meeting new people from different backgrounds. I decided I would begin my journey in the field of social services as a social worker, because I wanted to help and advocate on behalf of people who didn't have a voice. I started my curriculum in the field of liberal arts with a social science concentration. It was an exciting time for me because I was in school and making a deposit into my future; I was very proud of myself for striving to do better with my life. That semester I got all A's and made the dean's list every semester thereafter.

I loved going to Middlesex I was learning new things and thriving in school, but I was hard headed and couldn't get enough of the streets. I had one foot in my future and one foot in my past. Things were going smoothly or at least I thought, my demons still loomed in the back ground of my life. I was still hanging out smoking woolies here and there, hustling here and there, and trying to beat the probation system.

My probation officer Karen didn't bother me much because to her I was doing everything I needed to do. I wasn't tested as normal as other people, so it allowed for me to get high more frequently and that I did. Although I was in school and doing something with myself I hadn't worked on myself so I was doing the same thing with the same people and getting the same results, except this time I thought I was doing a little better because I was now in college.

It never dawned on me that I had a problem because I didn't look like I did drugs. I was naturally skinny and dressed nice, I was in school, and I was working. No way was I an addict, I didn't look or feel the part. I just loved to get drunk and high recreationally. This was the story I fed myself for years based on what my disease had me thinking until it became believable to me. I eventually completed probation and was happy not to have to worry about that system anymore. I was happy yet scared because I was moving full speed ahead. I was now living with my friend Adele and her mother on Madison Avenue in Perth Amboy while hustling and going to classes.

I can recall one Sunday afternoon Adele was going for a job interview and asked me to tag along. I was looking like death because I was up all night drinking and partying. I accompanied her on this interview for this debt collection agency in metro park, nj. While sitting there in the lobby the manager at the time Dave asked me if I wanted a job (hell yeah I thought to myself) and I responded yes I would. I filled out the application and was hired on the spot. I started working part time at JBC& Associates as a junior debt collector. I was happy because they paid $14 per hour and ShopRite wasn't cutting it anymore. I quit ShopRite and began working at JBC & Associates. I enjoyed working there because it was a fun and exciting environment. The hours were flexible and worked with my school schedule so it made it that much more fun working there. I met some amazing people while working there two of those people are my closest friends Renata and Qiana. I decided to move back home and stop hustling for a little while. I liked the direction I was moving in even if I was failing forward.

Although it seemed like I was moving in the right direction my demons still had control of me. I was excelling in college so nothing seemed out of the ordinary.

I partied hard on the weekends, worked hard during the week and did that continuously throughout college. During college I met a lot of people that helped piqued my interest in social activism (something that I grew to love). I was apart of a wonderful group known as AmeriCorps, which was spearheaded by Professor Donohue my political science professor at the time.

Professor Donohue was a sweet man who had a passion for social activism, he spoke highly of marches and protests he was apart of, the passion he brought to the classroom introduced me to the field of political science and its impact on society. What I was learning would help to shape my future so I was interested in working with him. I worked as a student aide employee under his leadership where I got paid to volunteer my time at the Amandla Crossing Transitional Home in Edison, NJ. I would go there and tutor small children in areas they lacked. That experience gave me a love for helping children and people. I learned a lot about AmeriCorps and went on national conventions with our group.

Our group was from all backgrounds of life, but the thread that held the fabric together was our willingness to help those less fortunate. I enjoyed that group because their mission was to help those in need and I took great pleasure in helping people in need. I wrestled with walking the right path and still being in the streets. I would be working on community activism yet still be in the streets hustling, smoking blunts and getting drunk. Apart of me didn't want to give up the street life because it was all I had come to know, but I was anxious in how my future was playing out before my eyes. Between hustling, school, partying, and working life as I understood it then was great.

This became the norm for me; As I mentioned before I didn't think I had any issues I just liked to have a good time on the weekends. I only came around on the weekends and I would hang out with my best friends Jennifer and Diana we would get drunk and go clubbing and then later I would sneak to the crack house to get high. Jennifer and I were always fighting and arguing with each other from the moment we met in middle school at Shull School. I used to be a jokester and always cracking on people including her. We would always fight and argue and speak back to each other the next day. I would be remiss to write this book and not mention the influence and impact Jennifer had on my life.

Jennifer and I share a bond that will always be unbreakable she will always be the light and love of my life. Jennifer has been there for me the entire ride, from the fights, to the laughter, to the hurts and pains that we've been through in life she has always been there for me no matter what, regardless of right or wrong. She was there for me through my addiction even when I tried to pretend that I was fine the love she had for me never waivered and she never treated me any different when she knew I was suffering from the disease of addiction.

I can vividly remember at my lowest point her and my dad beating down David's door looking for me when we were on one of our binges. Whatever I needed she took care of me, she played a pivotal role in my life through all aspects of my life. We are sisters and nothing will change that fact and for that I appreciate all the support she has given me. Her unwavering support is what fueled my motivation to want to change my life for the better. For that I thank you for being a friend.

Jennifer was always headstrong and protective of everyone around her from since we were 15 years old, she's still that way today and I wouldn't change anything about her. She was the mother figure out the group. If we planned anything she would have all the details and itinerary laid out as to how we approached our outing. Diana my other best friend was reserved and loved to have a good time without any drama. She and I were so carefree and never worried about anything we just wanted to have a good time, although I argued a lot with Jennifer it was the opposite with Diana, she was the calm between Jennifer and I. We knew everything about each other and still loved each other just the way we are. Our lives have evolved where they now have children so we connect when we can. I thank God for blessing me with amazing women to enjoy this journey with. So many women have paved the way for me and helped shaped the woman I am today. These are the women I consider my village and I love them all for just being an inspiration in my life.

CHAPTER TEN

Moving In the Wrong Direction

January 2003

I had officially graduated from Middlesex County College with an Associates degree in liberal arts with a concentration in social science. My intention was to become a social worker so I enrolled at Rutgers University and began immediately. I started Rutgers in the spring of 2003 as a junior and majored in Sociology with a minor in psychology. I knew that my life's purpose was to help those in need no matter what the capacity was. As my life began to progress so did the disease of addiction. I hadn't suffered any real consequences of my actions yet, so the partying got worst, the double life got worse, I was now introduced to the pipe and although I didn't like it at first, I liked the instant rush that it gave me, so from time to time I would indulge. I finally worked and got myself a brand new 2001 silver Honda accord coupe. I was the first one of my friends from the hood with a car aside from Jennifer; I would drive around everywhere just because I had a car.

Now that I had a car, the more I hung out and got drunk and high. One particular night that all caught up to me. I was out drinking at a bar in Perth Amboy, I was having a good time at Shorty's bar drinking long island ice teas all night and dancing enjoying the music I was so fucked up that I assumed I was able to drive. I mapped out how I would end my night by going to the crack house which is what I did frequently when I went out partying. A chick I was partying with asked me to take her home to South Amboy, which was the next town over I said yes not realizing how drunk I was and off we went.

I made it to South Amboy and dropped her off safely. On my way back I fell into a black out state and all I could remember was turning onto a street and side swiping cars before I knew it I crashed on someone's lawn and kept driving, I was so consumed with going to see the coke dealer that I never paid any attention to the damage I was causing as I was driving. As I'm approaching the victory bridge, which by the way is a huge bridge that connects the surrounding towns to Perth Amboy. I got pulled over by the South Amboy Police.

I was so drunk that they had to pull me out the car; I was driving on three wheels with a broken axle and never knew it. My blood alcohol level was close to dead. I was arrested and brought to jail; this would now be my second dui on record. I mustered up the courage and called my best friend Jennifer to come and get me she was always my rescue. The next morning was a blur to me I didn't remember anything which was the usual case for me at this point in my life. I had become a black out drunk every time I drank.

Jennifer replayed the night for me based on what the cops told her. They told her had I gone over that bridge I would have died; my alcohol level was about three times over the legal limit at the time of my arrest. I was embarrassed to say the least and didn't want my parent's to know. I self medicated as a coping mechanism to deal with the consequences. My life was spinning out of control fast and I didn't care. I still did the same things as if nothing happened.

My relationship with my parents was pretty much non existent at this point. I felt that they hated me. We spoke less and I was rude and belligerent to them because my behavior was changing due to the increase in my drug use. Now I'm smoking coke more frequently to take the edge off of my drinking. It was as if I was on a hamster wheel and couldn't get off. My life was officially spinning out of control, but I continued working, going to school and studying hard. During the weekend I was a totally different person. I would binge on drugs from Friday to Sunday. I had met some addicts in Rahway and began hanging out in their basement smoking the pipe. I really didn't like going there but I knew that I could score drugs no matter the hour if I went there, so every weekend like clock work I was there, it was like a mini club so many different people would be in different parts of the basement getting high. I hated that because I just wanted to take a hit and space out, but that was never the case because I always got nervous around different people. I would begin to hallucinate and imagine hearing noises and just sit frozen in the same spot until the next morning.

When my money ran out they would ask me to leave. I hated the way I felt once I came down from my cocaine induced high because I was now left to deal with the feelings of self loathing, self pity, low self esteem, hundreds of dollars in bank overdrafts and the fact that I may have an issue. From time to time I thought about ending it all, but I knew that was something that I couldn't bring myself to do. This was a very dark period in my life because I didn't understand the nature of how my disease operated I just knew that I somehow may have a problem even if I only went on weekend binges.

My disease always reminded me that I was fine and nothing was wrong with me. I wasn't a bum; I worked, went to school and had my own car. No way was I an addict I just liked partying on the weekends, but deep down inside I knew I had a problem I just didn't know the extent of it. I was in the grips of my addiction and couldn't stop using.

My parents couldn't figure out what was wrong with me. I was losing weight, always depressed, coming and going. It wasn't until they started finding burnt up soda cans in my room that my dad approached me and asked me if I had a problem because he had seen the burnt cans on TV that was used as paraphernalia to smoke crack. I vehemently denied his accusation with a straight face and asked him how he could accuse me of these things. I told him some crazy shit as to why the cans were under my bed, I don't think he ever believed me; the pain behind his eyes told me he didn't believe me. I was off to the races and nothing could stop me.

With my using at an all time high God is still blessing me with new opportunities. School was coming along fine; my grades were great, I had a good job working for the temp agency as a receptionist for a mortgage company, and then I got the call in January 2004 to come in for an interview with a major utility company here in New Jersey. I was excited and wasn't going to mess up this opportunity. I stopped smoking and drinking and laid low for a few weeks until I got the job. After a month of paperwork and drug testing I finally landed the job on February 24, 2004.

I can remember the conversation with my dad like it was yesterday. My dad knew I smoked a lot of weed and whatever else I ingested and he was adamant on me getting this job. The night before, I took quick flush to flush my system, apparently my dad didn't trust that the quick flush would work so the next morning he made me drink vinegar straight and chase it with cranberry juice. By the time I got to the testing facility to take my drug test I damn neared peed on myself, between the quick flush and the vinegar my pee was the color of water needless to say I passed the drug test and was excited for my future. I was happy to finally land a real job. My dad was more excited for me than I was because lord knows I was tired of working temp jobs. I told myself I would lay off the drugs because with this position I'd be making a lot more money and hopefully the potential to grow with this awesome company.

I went through training excited to learn and grow in my new position. I asked questions, gained insight and clarity on certain functions of their system. I was in training for close to six months and in that time frame I was doing well with keeping my disease at bay. Once I got out of training I started in the position and quickly saw that this isn't what I thought it was, I was met with disorganization and an archaic management style system. One hand didn't know what the other was doing; I knew instantly that I wouldn't be here long enough for them to get to know me. I worked in a call center environment as a customer service representative. The pay was worth every bit of the aggravation and headache the job entailed. I spoke with angry customers all day everyday. I couldn't wait to get home and get high. I worked the night shift for the first 5 years while on the job. This was perfect for me in terms of school and my recreational habit.

I was a few semesters shy of graduating from Rutgers with my bachelor's degree when I landed this job. I wasn't sure if this was the job I wanted or needed.

The department was very lackadaisical and lacked any good leadership so to speak. One hand never knew what the other was doing. I figured it was the perfect marriage for my addiction, no one knew me in the beginning. I came and went was very quiet and never showed up on the weekends, my addiction came first on the weekends. That happened for some time until I was spoken to about my availability at work; I put the water works on and promised to do better, that never really happened. So as I went through the motions at this job, I really began to feel like I was trapped. I wanted to do more with my life but I was held hostage by my disease. The hours where perfect even though I wasn't sure if I was the right fit for this job, I liked the money because it fueled my addiction. I was always broke but always managed to pay my bills on time.

As I navigated the nuances of the job I met some pretty amazing people. Many of my coworkers were talented individuals that do outstanding things within there communities and outside the workplace. I'm thankful for my job because it allowed me to meet some wonderful people that I consider apart of my village. It's so many to name that have helped me along the way that have prayed for me, supported me in everything that I do, that have been there for me and have been a true friend to me. These amazing people have become my second family. I'm thankful to those that really know my story and all that I have been through. A job that I hated originally I grew to love the culture and people. Speaking of people there is one specifically that changed the course of my life forever.

CHAPTER ELEVEN

An Enigmatic Love

I was on my job for over a year and a half when I met David we both worked the night shift and became cool. He was nice, attentive, quiet and cute to me. He also seemed to have a genuine interest in me, I couldn't figure out why, because I had very low self esteem at the time and thought if he really knew who I was he would haul ass, so I just rolled with it like whatever. I figured I would hang out with him, sleep with him, and ignore him. That didn't happen. He actually liked me. We talked a lot on the phone hung out without having sex; he was nice, courteous, charming and chivalrous. We went on dates, something I wasn't used to. We would do simple things like go to the movies, or the mall and walk around or go and grab something to eat. It was cute and new to me and I liked it. He knew nothing about my addiction and I liked it that way. The more we spent time together I think he thought I was a saint, but only if he knew the real me. I was determined not to let him get to know the real me, because I was afraid he wouldn't like me, so I captured his mind with my intelligence and my ability to be engaging and loving and before I knew it he was under my spell.

One day in conversation I told him my deep dark secret and of course I lied and minimized my drug use to something I did here and there, surprisingly he was accepting of it and told me he dabbled here and there. A big sigh of relief overcame me and from that day forward we rocked and rolled for five long hard tumultuous years. Our love was reminiscent of bobby and whitney during their highs and lows.

When I met David I was still attending Rutgers and just moved to Old Bridge NJ, I was in my very first apartment and I was excited. I finally moved out my parents' house and was doing the grown up thing. I remembered having a house warming and I stupidly invited my coworkers to my house warming. We were all chilling, drinking, and smoking. David got drunk and started causing a scene, this was the first time I seen him act this way.

He was drunk and mumbling incoherent things I couldn't understand. We started fighting and I cracked him over the head with my new lamp, blood starting gushing from his head, I was scared but in the meantime I wanted him to know I wasn't to be fucked with. The fight got a little out of control and the cops were called, when the cops got there I knew nothing, saw nothing, said nothing (code of the streets), people started disappearing and just like that the party was over. I ended up going to Rahway to get high that night and the rest of the weekend. I didn't speak to him for the rest of the weekend until I got to work on Monday.

When I got to work on Monday I was the talk of the office. People gossiped about my housewarming all throughout the office. I was embarrassed and ashamed, but in the same breath didn't really give a fuck. I didn't know those people and they didn't know me. The funny thing about gossip is when the tables are turned on you and you're the one being talked about, it doesn't feel good. I didn't like being the talk of the office, but I held my head high. I think from that moment forward my coworkers knew I was crazy.

This relationship with David was new to me and boundaries were being tested and needed to be set. I never saw David in that drunken state before, and I wasn't impressed but I believed in giving him a second chance. I dismissed it as him just being drunk. We talked about it and moved forward in our relationship. Never once did I think this was the beginning of a volatile relationship. As we progressed in our relationship we were always the topic of gossip. I was being talked about and judged by my coworkers for being with him. I didn't believe our relationship was toxic, we were just two crazy kids in love or so I thought. People would make snide comments about him and I. Honestly, I believed it was love, because that's what I thought love looked and felt like. I was walking around in lot of emotional pain and the only way I knew how to manage that pain was to self-medicate and lash out.

I hated the direction my life was going in. I was estranged from my parents once again. My father never liked David from the day he met him, I don't know whether it was the parental instinct but my dad didn't like that he had so much influence over his daughter. I knew he tried for my sake to like him, but he just couldn't bring himself to. I was in love and thought things were perfect between him and I. I slowly began to see his controlling effects play out over the course of our relationship. I thought I could change his ways if I loved him more, remained faithful and loyal to him, but that wasn't enough this man wanted my soul. He didn't trust me and he reminded me of that whenever he got drunk or high.

The years came by fast and our drug use escalated in the blink of an eye. I no longer hung out with strange people in basements or with friends to get high, because I now got high with him, and I liked using with him at first because I no longer hid my secret, it wasn't until our usage escalated that I started to see a different side of him.

David had a Jekyll and Hyde personality when he drank. I hated him because of the things he would say or do when he was high. He would take a hit and start searching me like he was the dam cops. I hated that shit because when I took a hit I wanted to be left alone and hide out in the bathroom and he was always bothering me. Plenty of nights I literally had to claw him off of me because for some odd reason he thought I was hiding a stash or whatever. When he was sober I loved him because he was thoughtful, caring, nurturing, and made sure I was good in every sense of the word. Our chemistry was out of this world it was this weird sort of enigmatic love we had for each other. We were both detrimental to each other, because no matter what we couldn't get enough of each other, we loved each other and were each other's best friend's. Aside from the drug use we talked a lot about getting and staying clean to help each other, me finishing school, and us moving the relationship to the next level.

In the midst of being in the grips of our addiction we were moving along in our relationship and decided we would move in with each other. My lease was up in the old bridge apartment and because I was on my second dui from the South Amboy incident I now had to have the interlock device installed in my car as part of my suspended sentence. My license and registration were suspended for two years and I had to take motor vehicle classes in order to get my license back.

The interlock device was a breathalyzer device that the state of NJ installed in my car as part of my sentence. The device itself required the driver to blow into the mouthpiece on the device in order to start the car. I was too afraid to be driving back and forth from Newark to old bridge on a suspended license so we decided to move in together to cut cost and be able to better move around. I enjoyed living in Newark. It was close to my job, was in a pretty decent neighborhood in the weequahic section of Newark and the drug dealers were always out. Things were good for the first few months. I made the apartment look and feel like home by decorating it with the furniture and paintings I had in my house. The apartment finally started to feel like home and we were working and putting our best foot forward.

I was in my last semester and schedule to graduate from Rutgers in the May of 2005. Everything was going according to plan. The night before I was set to graduate from Rutgers University we were up all night partying. The next morning I made it just in time to graduate. I looked a hot disheveled mess, but my mom and dad was there beaming with pride along with my nephew, sister, and a few of my friends. That day meant a lot to me and David didn't show up for me, I chalked it up to him being hung over, but I still couldn't shake the feeling that he hadn't shown up for me. David's absence at my graduation hurt my feelings and left me feeling angry and upset, but I hid my feelings and enjoyed my graduation festivities.

That night I got drunk and went out with my friends Jennifer and Diana to celebrate my graduation. We went to a comedy club in Nyc. I had on a pink corduroy jacket with matching corduroy pants to match with a white camisole underneath. We got to the comedy show and I remembered sitting close to the front row. I was drunk and heckling and calling the comedian all kinds of names. He began making horrible jokes about me being black and skinny and that "I looked liked a ghetto power ranger". Although it was all in fun my feelings were hurt because the attention was on me and people were laughing at me. I was laughing too to distract them from really seeing the pain in my eyes but I really wanted to crawl under a rock at that very moment. That night I tried to play it off like I had a great time but I wanted to hurry back to David's house and get high to escape the emotional pain I was in.

I got back to David's house that night and all I wanted to do was get high to escape the laughter and jokes that were still dancing in my head. I was still hurting from him not showing up to my graduation, from being a disappointment to myself, from being laughed at and all I wanted to do was get high. I was angry at the fact that David would tell me he loved me and never showed up for me to something that was important for me. That sent mix signals to my brain. I tried to downplay the situation by telling myself he didn't have a car, he was tired, and every other excuse in the book, but I was hurting inside. I eventually forgave him but I never forgot how his absence at my graduation made me feel.

CHAPTER TWELVE

In the Grips of
My Addiction

I enrolled at Nathan Weiss Graduate School at Kean University in spring of 2005. My degree would be concentrated in the area of Healthcare Administration under the Public Administration umbrella. I began my normal studies and absolutely hated that campus compared to Rutgers world class campus, however I did love that I was in close proximity to my job and my home in Newark. My first core courses were intro courses to public administration. I had no interest in the course work but I managed to make it through the semester. In addition to going to Kean for my graduate studies I was also going to motor vehicle classes that were mandated by the state in order to get my license back. Everything was working in my favor, but the monkey didn't stay off my back for too long. I was a terrible enabler and would talk David into using because I wanted to or felt I should be rewarded for doing what I was supposed to be doing. So we would start back up and within weeks we would be back out of work again chasing the pipe. I hated when we fell off track because it would be hard to get us back on track. In my head I wanted a happy home and I knew we couldn't have that if we were both using and enabling each other.

I want to be very clear about sharing this part of my story. In no way shape or form am I defaming David's character because he was an amazing friend and lover however this was a pivotal part of my addiction because not only was I addicted to the drugs, I was also addicted to him which made everything worst. He was my drug of choice and the fact that I could use with him brought about a level of trust between us that no one could or would understand. Plenty of times people told him to leave me and vice versa but we loved each other and trusted each other with our deepest darkest secrets and that's what kept us together. Every time I attempted to get clean I would go back for David to try and get him clean. It never worked in my favor because I was always high before I could get him clean. I started going to a Spiritual Program to try and get my using under control, it would work for a few weeks and I'd pick up again and be off to the races.

What I learned in the Spiritual Program is that everyone's process is their own. I can't get and stay clean and try to save someone else. I would be high again before I would be clean. Through research and development I found that to be true. I would drag him to meetings and two days later we would be using and I couldn't figure out what I was doing wrong. The relationship turned volatile because the drugs were pulling us in two different directions. I was now becoming tired of entering in and out of rehab facilities, in and out of the Spiritual Program and not being able to function on my job. I was already a disappointment in my parent's eyes. I was constantly lying and dramatizing everything. I wanted to change for the better, but I didn't know how to begin. I was in and out of outpatient programs, Spiritual Program, church and nothing was working for me.

My first semester of graduate school was a success I had gotten all A's in all four classes so I celebrated by getting high. School in general was important to me because as I mentioned earlier it made me feel normal. It was the only thing that made me feel like I was worthy; it was also something I was good at. I was sick and suffering at the hands of my addiction and found solace in my education. I loved learning new things. I can never explain how my brain shifted on and off when I was in and out the classroom. I was a scholar and always felt at peace in school it was my way of escaping everything that was going on in my life. The crazy thing is I would be doing my thesis paper and getting high at the same time. I honestly do not know how I managed to get through graduate school with a little under 4.0 grade point average. I loved when the weekends arrived because my plan of action consisted of me getting high from Friday to Sunday. By Monday I would be depressed and crawling out my skin.

My drug use was out of control I was less than one hundred pounds and looked and felt like death, I started missing more days at work and I wasn't able to function anymore. I was in and out of my Spiritual Program meetings trying to get clean. I would go 3 days without using and be fatigued, irritable, and ready to kill anyone. My disease had progressed so badly that the anticipation leading up to the ingestion of coke had my stomach in knots my palms would start shaking and become sweaty. I would be shaking and my stomach would be in knots preceded by me having the runs until I took a hit. Once

I took a hit I would be frozen in time as if the world stopped. I would begin to hallucinate and every sound was magnified, I would zero in on everything on the floor. It was as if I was in a zombie like trance.

I began using daily and feeding myself the same excuse over and over again. My excuse was that I could only take a hit and ill be good. I would get off work on pay day go to the liquor store buy drugs and be up until the next morning, once the depression set in, I couldn't or wouldn't go to work, this cycle was repeated day after day, week after week, season after season. I got to the point that I became suicidal because I just couldn't keep up anymore. I was wearing too many masks and I was simply tired. I would come to work in the same dingy oversized white tee shirt. When I was there I was useless, irritable, and downright nasty. My relationship was stagnant, to be honest, I was content with David because I knew no one else wanted me hell I didn't even want me. Our relationship got to the point where it was strictly about drugs. I didn't like using by myself so I hung out with him and quite honestly I was ok with it because all I wanted to do was get high.

I suffered a lot of emotional and verbal abuse from David. In many ways, he reminded me of my father when my father drank. Depending on David's mood when he drank I was either a ugly black bitch that no one wanted or I was the love of his life, I was used to his tirades and expletives by now and actually believed every word he said because it had been told to me all my life. The abuse got worse sooner than later, we partied more and more and fought more and more. Our fights turned physical quickly. On more than one occasion I wore a few black eyes and bruises.

I can remember one Christmas we didn't exchange any gifts and we had been getting high all day into the night. We got into an argument and he locked me out his house, here I am in the hallway with half my clothes on geeking out banging on the door and he would turn up the music on the stereo to drown out the banging on the door. This wasn't his first time doing these embarrassing things to me, and of course I still wanted to be around him and continue to get high. Oftentimes when he would put me out I would climb onto the fire escape to try and get into the apartment and he would push me back out the window, where I would fall down the fire escape, I felt stupid, embarrassed, and depressed because I knew deep down inside that love wasn't suppose to be this way or feel like this. When he decided to throw my belongings out the window I would leave angry, upset, and defeated wanting to get high. I believed he got a kick out of doing evil shit to me when he was drunk and high. The funny thing is I would be right back at his house the next day looking to get high. I was addicted to him and the drugs and would tolerate anything to just get one more. The fights were now a common occurrence.

One Friday night we had been getting drunk and high per usual and we started fighting because like I said earlier he had a tendency to start searching me whenever he took a hit, this particular night however, he began searching me and I was fighting him off of me and he blacked out and started fighting me and calling me all kinds of whores and that he knew I was sleeping with other people. The look in his eyes as his words penetrated my soul was that of a mad man. In that moment I felt as though he was trying to kill me, for the first time I was scared, and didn't know what to do. I called the cops and when they arrived he started talking shit to them and trying to fight them. He was arrested and put in jail; I took that opportunity to move out of his house while he was locked up.

I rented a U-Haul truck and got my father to help me get everything out of David's place while he was locked up. I put my stuff in storage and began staying with my friend Magreta for a few weeks until I found a place in Edison New Jersey. I moved into the apartment and got settled, at this time he had gotten out of jail and he was upset that I moved out, although we were still together the beginning of the end was imminent. The relationship changed drastically and I knew that it was a matter of time before we would go our separate ways. He hated my new place because he couldn't keep tabs on me like he did when we lived together. He hated to come over, so naturally I was always at his house getting high per usual, however something felt different I didn't look at him the same anymore I didn't have the same feelings I had for him anymore it was strictly about the drugs.

CHAPTER THIRTEEN

Growing Pains

I was growing tired and scared to be around David because it was always physical and verbal abuse. We were both sick, we began to sell whatever we could out of my house just to get high because truth be told we had stopped going to work and we weren't getting paid anymore. I hated to get high with him because I didn't know who he would become when he got high; it was a chance I'd have to take if I wanted to get high with him. I started getting high by myself because he was annoying and the pain of my addiction was starting to become unbearable, I couldn't focus on work anymore nor could

I keep myself awake in classes anymore, I had become pathetic and depressed. I tried the spiritual program on several occasions and I would want to get help but didn't know how to. I would go and share and cry about wanting to stay clean and I would use the minute I came out of a meeting. In school I had a story for every assignment that was due, but oddly enough I kept on with A's so I kept on partying.

I still had the interlock device in my car and I was growing tired of having it, because it stopped by flow. Every time I got in the car I had to blow in the breathalyzer in order to start the car. How does that work with 2 addicts, it was disastrous and embarrassing, but we became creative by asking people to blow into it and figuring out how long we had to get from one destination to the other between blows. We did this for awhile, after 3 times of bad readings the device automatically locked the car. The car wouldn't start and I had to take it to tom's river to get it re-calibrated. It was a headache and exhausting. I don't know how I got through that phase but I did.

With all the hits I had been taken lately I was excited that my graduation was fastly approaching in a few short months and I was partying harder than ever with David. I was scheduled to walk across the stage to get my master's degree on May 15, 2008. I was down to my final stretch and still felt worthless, ashamed, and suicidal. I couldn't believe that the semester was finally coming to a close and I would obtain my masters degree. I was excited, to think that I actually did it even with my using at an all time high. What was supposed to be a joyous occasion was riddled with self doubt and self loathing. I hated myself, my parents on the other hand were happy that I was graduating. Even though I was estranged from my parents they never missed an opportunity to support me in whatever I was doing. They were my biggest cheerleader and they kept me in their prayers.

The night before my graduation I was up all night partying. I slept most of the day and arrived at my graduation later that evening out of sync, and just not looking my best. I tried to pretend like I was doing great and was excited, but I was depressed and looked the part. My parents, although happy for my accomplishments knew that I was sick. I could see the pain, disappointment, and frustration behind their eyes, especially my dad. He knew I was struggling with staying clean. David again never showed up to my graduation and I knew that it would be over shortly after this. David not showing up to my graduation brought about a feeling of hurt that is hard to explain, we were together for five years at this point and been through hell and back together. For him not to support something that meant so much to me again was the beginning of the end for me.

I had given my soul to this man and never once did he support me in anything that I attempted to do. We had conversations about him not attending my first graduation, but I don't think he really understood the magnitude of how I truly felt. I never told him how I felt because in my mind I knew the relationship was done and I was tired of him manipulating the situation to his benefit. Instead I quickly retreated inward and began to internalize my feelings which lead to my exacerbated drug use. I was spiritually bankrupt and hated everything about my life. How could someone that claimed to love me so much not support something that meant a great deal to me, I mean I was graduating from graduate school this was a magnamimous accomplishment for me considering how hard I worked to get my degree. I pretty much concluded that he just never cared that much about it.

I understand that he was intimidated with me at times, but that wasn't an excuse to miss my second graduation ceremony. He knew how important my education meant to me and my graduation was just as important. We had talked about him attending my graduation ceremony weeks in advance where he promised me he would be there front and center with me since he missed the first one. David not showing up left me feeling disappointed and angry for all the times he never showed up for me while in the relationship.

David used to tell me that when I graduated I would leave him or no other man would want me. The truth be told I didn't want to leave him I just wanted to fix him, but deep down inside I knew I couldn't fix him. The verbal abuse was now becoming exhausting and unbearable for me to deal with. He was emotionally manipulative and I was growing tired of the negativity. Things were slowly taking its course and the end was impending. I was no longer happy with him or around him. He made me feel less than and inadequate all the time. In my heart I knew I deserved better I just didn't think I was worth better.

There was so much external and internal conflict that was happening to me I couldn't make sense of anything anymore. With all the chaos happening with me

David got fired from the job we worked at together. I was hurt that he was terminated because he was a great employee when he was sober and he showed up to work, but apart of me was relieved, I knew deep down inside that I wanted to get clean and I couldn't if we continued to work together and use together. The fights were continuous and work was becoming strenuous, I hated being there, when I was there I struggled to be productive.

Another incident that shaped the course of my destiny was an incident that occurred between me and a supervisor at the time. I was working my regular shift which was from 3-1130pm. On this particular day in December right around Christmas I came to work early on overtime at 10am. Some time after noon I had just finished wrapping up a call with a customer and pressed the wrap button on the phone system. The wrap button prevents calls from coming in once I got off a call. I must've been in wrap for a very long time, because the supervisor that was supervising the podium was beeping me and yelling my name to get my attention. I became easily fatigued and irritated and flew into a fit of rage. A part of me believed it was due in part to me not using drugs in a few days because I was easily fatigued and irritable. I became irate yelling at him asking him why was he beeping me, can't he see that I was doing something. We went back and forth arguing and it ignited like a fire. I invited him outside to fight. I was a loose cannon that day. Once I was calmed down by my union representatives I continued on into my shift as if nothing happened.

As the evening approached I went on my lunch break and smoked a blunt with one of my coworkers to take the edge off of me from all that had transpired earlier in the day. As soon as I came back from my lunch break I was immediately brought into an investigatory meeting and drug tested on the spot. Unbeknownst to me that exchange from earlier between me and the on duty supervisor resulted in me being brought into this investigatory meeting about my actions form earlier.

Everything was done sneakily and without my k[...]edge. I was sent home on administrative leave wi[...]out pay until the results of the drug test came back. It would take a while because it was the holiday season and let's face it why would they rush when I wasn't getting paid. The company already knew I had a history of drug abuse because I took advantage of their EAP (Employee Assistance Program) program so what I believed to be confidential wasn't.

This was leverage for them to test me without it being warranted. I went home that night scared because I wasn't sure if cocaine would show up in my system or if I would be fired for my latest antics. So many thoughts were running through my mind What if they found coke in my system? What if I get fired? What's going to happen to me? All these thoughts permeated my mind and I was scared. I did what I knew best and that was to get high.

On Christmas day I bought a copious amount of cocaine and alcohol. The intention was to kill myself. I ny rope and hated who I was. I went

d retrieved one of those small steak

st once I started partying. I used all

ours of the morning by myself. I was

delusional, hiding under the table and running from my

own shadow by this point. I began hallucinating, crying,

shaking, pacing back and forth ready to end my life. I put

the knife to my wrist and I just couldn't bring myself to

slitting my wrist. I began to cry out to God to help me

please. My cry for help was loud and sincere because in

that moment I was defeated and knew that if I continued

to use I would die. My addiction had won I was spiritu-

ally and emotionally bankrupt. I had hit my rock bottom.

I prayed and asked God to save my life and in that

moment I believed he answered and saved me. I heard a

loud voice that said "enough". I looked around in the dark

room scared to turn on the lights because I was so high I

was hiding from my own shadow. I was high and geeking

out so I thought the voice was from my imagination and

maybe it was but I heard that voice loud and clear. The voice got louder and now I'm really scared I'm standing in the dark frozen with a knife in one hand and the pipe in my other hand sweating profusely trying to hide from my shadow. I'm shaking and crying not sure if it was because I was scared, high, or sincerely tired, but I knew this was the end for me. It felt like the walls were closing in on me.

I fell to my knees and began to pray for help and asking God for forgiveness and to please save me. I ended up crying myself to sleep on the floor. This was what my rock bottom looked and felt like. In the end I was alone, isolated, depressed, ashamed, guilt ridden, and trapped in my own home. I was hallucinating, delusional, and scared of my own damn shadow. I knew deep done in my soul that this was the end of the road for me. That night when I cried out to God and sincerely asked him to save my life I felt something shift in me and in that moment God did just what I prayed to him for because that was the last time I used alcohol and drugs. It was December 26th, 2008.

CHAPTER FOURTEEN

Afraid of the Unknown

The next morning I got up and got rid of all the paraphernalia from the night before. I threw everything in the trash, cleaned my house and called up a friend that I had met in the Spiritual Program. I started going back to my Spiritual Program and really relied on the program to carry me. I knew some people that I had met from coming in and out the rooms so it was easy to call them to help me whenever I got stuck. I signed myself into an outpatient program and made the Spiritual Program my home. I began to work the spiritual program, making 90 meetings in 90 days, getting a sponsor, getting a commitment (I was the coffee maker), sharing at meetings, and working my steps. I ended things with David because in my heart I knew the relationship had to end if I wanted to save my life. I wanted to save my life more than make the relationship work. Gradually the relationship ended. I stayed away from people, places, and things and focused on staying clean. I ended up coming back to work about 2 months later and was placed on 36 months probation with random drug testing, which was fine as long as I kept my job.

There were days I wanted to use more than I wanted to stay clean, but I went to meetings and shared about my urges. I learned a lot during early recovery. I learned that I used because of my feelings and that I need to be cognizant of things that triggered me to use. I grew close to God and I prayed everyday and still do to this day always thanking him for keeping me clean. Its just apart of my prayer. I met God in the Spiritual Program. I knew who God was but our relationship developed in the Spiritual

Program. I relied on him for everything and in doing so I was able to witness miracles on his behalf.

Things were starting to look up for me. I made 90 meetings in 90 days and challenged myself to make another 90 meetings in 90 days and so forth. I stayed around people in the Spiritual Program. I wanted what these people had which was peace, serenity, love, and hope. I was making meetings and in the process I started to feel good about myself my weight had picked up and my skin had cleared up immensely. I was ready to move forward with my new life.

I began looking for a home and within two months of looking for a home I found my condo. I was already preapproved for a home loan and bought my first condo in March of 2009, ninety days after being clean. I don't remember any thing about how I got this condo. I didn't pay anything for this condo meaning I was approved for grants from the state which was used towards the down payment and closing cost of the condo. It was a nice condo in a quiet development in North Brunswick NJ. Looking back with a set of different eyes I can see that this was nothing but God's grace and mercy telling me to trust him and the process. I'm so glad I trusted him. Like I said I don't know how I got that condo, but what I do know is that God was showering me with blessings after blessings.

I moved into the condo and became enamored in fixing up my new home, David and I had split amicably. I was single, making meetings, surrounding myself with the right people and I felt great about myself. I started to learn a lot about myself like what I really liked to do as oppose to what everyone else liked to do. I found out I liked Italian food, my favorite colors are red and purple and that I had a hidden gift of interior designing in addition to being rather stylish. I put down the drugs and started picking up other habits like shopping, interior design, and fashion. I realized once I got clean I would spend my money on shopping. It was my rationality for staying clean. I substituted one drug habit for a shopping habit; I always had a rationale for spending money on clothes. I was doing great and feeling great. I mended my relationship with my parents and began to earn their trust again.

My dad saw the changes in me and couldn't have been more pleased and proud with how I was working on turning my life around. He told me how proud he was of me and that all he wanted for me was to get myself together. That meant a great deal to me because for so long I had disappointed both my parents and I wanted to make it up to them. I continued on in my recovery and for awhile things were just complacent. I wasn't dating I was working and going to meetings, working on my steps and meeting new people whenever time permitted.

I've had the pleasure of meeting many great people that have been in my corner, however along the way I met lifelong friends such as Qiana and Renata in addition to the village of women I currently have in my life. I met both ladies when I started working at JBC & Associates during college we had an instant connection that spans almost two decades of friendship, they totally get my crazy. To this day we are the best of friends with the inclusion of yet another great friend Cynthia. Cynthia and I met later on in life around 2009-2010 we instantly hit it off. When I met her I automatically saw this beautiful goddess. She was smart, kind, beautiful, comedic, had skin like cocoa, and had ratchet tendencies like me. I loved her instantly.

We met through Qiana and my women's organization Musuyanama she was a member at the time. She reminded me of my self smart, sure of ourselves, thoughtful, funny, secure in some areas of our lives, fun loving, head strong, and self less. We shared a lot of similarities in our lives. We were both single, like to travel, struggling to some degree within certain areas of our lives so it was easy for us to connect and that we did. We have been by each others side since day one. These are the women I surround myself around and bounced my ideas off of. These women loved me until I learned how to love my self. They are an amazing group of women that I am blessed to have in my life. I'm grateful and thankful to have the pleasure of having a seat at their table in this thing called life.

CHAPTER FIFTEEN

Back to Life

By mid 2010 I was focused on my recovery and bettering myself when I met a man named Lawrence on Facebook. Lawrence inboxed me out of the blue telling me how beautiful I was. I said thank you although I didn't believe him. My self esteem was very low at the time I met Lawrence. I couldn't see what he saw in me. I figured if he saw how smart I was he would fall in love with me. I really liked Lawrence like nervous liked him. I would be so nervous around him my palms and underarms would be sweating whenever I was in his presence. One of the things that caught my attention was the level of intelligence he had. I thought he was handsome and well spoken, plus he had a bald head which was my weakness. He asked me questions about what books I've read, which I thought was interesting because no one ever asked me those kinds of questions before. At the time I was reading the autobiography of Malcolm X and we had an amazing conversation on his life and legacy. I thought wow he's really smart. Those were some of the talking points that we shared during our initial conversations when we were getting to know each other. I was automatically drawn to this sapiosexual man. I thanked God repeatedly for sending me an amazingly handsome, intelligent and well versed man. I was instantly turned on by him.

Lawrence was different from David he didn't use drugs or smoke, he wasn't what I was used to he was nice, charming, handsome and reserved. I fell for him instantly, we went out on a few dates that I can remember and we hit it off, but for some reason I think he sensed my insecurities early on and played into them. I was always nervous when I was around him, and felt that I wasn't enough for him. I was always trying to be someone else based on what he liked. The shit drove me crazy. We became sexual and fell into a situation-ship status, but in my head I thought we were in a relationship. Blame it on me being naïve and gullible, but it seemed like he was always too busy whenever I tried to spend time with him, but never busy enough to sleep with me when his schedule permitted.

He was good at manipulating the conversation whenever I brought up how I felt about the way I was being treated. It was always turned around on me where my feelings were reduced and I was made to think that I was crazy for even insinuating anything, he was very smooth with it and I didn't pick up on it until after our situation ended. We never did anything together other than the few dates we went on when we first met. I never met his family. I was a side chick and when questioned of course he denied it. (He tells me otherwise) but I now know better. I carried on this situation with Lawrence for more than a year and I really was in love and blinded by his smooth talking ways. He was emotionally manipulative something I knew nothing of when dealing with him. I just know that I would always question myself after speaking with him. He was always busy with all his extracurricular activities. I would watch him on Facebook when he had all his function for his organization and he never once invited me to anything except a party or two. I wanted so much for him to love me and see me for who I was but he never did.

Lawrence had a way of making me weak even when he told me things that weren't the truth. He would always remark that he loved me but his actions never matched the words that came out of his mouth. Whenever I asked him was I a side chick he would tell me no and make this long drawn out point to prove I wasn't and I believed him. Matter of fact I believed anything he told me because I wanted him to love me and see me for who I was. Lawrence was a single man who operated under those pretenses; but somehow I couldn't see that because I was searching tirelessly for love. It never dawned on me that love didn't feel like this. I figured since he didn't use drugs we could have a shot. It never failed whenever I met a guy I automatically had a picture of our wedding in my head. This clouded my judgment because I didn't realize how difficult dating was. I was naïve, gullible, and easily manipulated.

While I was doing everything to make sure this man would like me, he only saw me as a convenient piece of ass from time to time. Life lessons are best looked at when you are removed from a situation or overcome an obstacle. I look back and compare where I am today and know that I would have never dealt with Lawrence in that capacity, but it was necessary for me to have these experiences in order to blossom into the bold and fearless woman I am today. I thank God for these lessons because they have shaped who I am today.

The same way I met Lawrence is the same way I knew he was involved with another woman. We had spoken and he told me he was preparing to go on vacation with his friends. Seeing that we were friends on Facebook I was able to see his tagged photos. I was able to find her entire life within a few hours. I stalked her page and learned she was an attorney and automatically felt myself being reduced to shit, because I automatically assumed she was better than me because of her title.

They had this whirlwind romance where they went on vacation and I saw the pictures. I inboxed her to tell her about Lawrence's extracurricular activities with me and about his lies. I was made to look like a desperate woman according to her and what he had told her about me. We had a conversation where she told me what I already suspected; needless to say I left that situation alone and never looked back. He was upset and said a few choice words to me. I was devastated and my heart was broken into pieces. That was the first time I ever experienced heartache. My heart was literally broken. I never experienced that kind of pain before.

At the time I had a clothing boutique in linden, NJ. I was so heartbroken the pain alone made me sick that I had to close my shop for a few days to recuperate. I thank god for my best friend Magreta who was working with me at the time. She kept it together for me. I stayed in bed for three days and didn't eat for a week. I was literally dead. The pain I felt in my heart was if someone literally pulled my heart out of my chest and broke it in half. I prayed to God to help me get through this heartache. This was the first time I ever experienced heartbreak of this magnitude. I never experienced that with David, and that was due in part because I knew that the relationship that I had with David was rooted in addiction, but with Lawrence for some reason what I felt was real was nothing more than an illusion.

Lawrence wasn't a bad guy however I will say that he never had any intentions of being more than bed buddies with me regardless of what he told me. He talked a great game and was good at manipulating the situation to make it seem like I was crazy. I never had an encounter with a man like that so I quickly began to think I was making things up and that my mind was playing tricks on me. That wasn't the case he was a master manipulator and once I woke up and seen him for who he was I was no longer interested in entertaining him any longer.

This experience with Lawrence toughened me up because I started accepting myself for who I was and stopped trying to be someone I wasn't. After a few months I started feeling good about myself. My prayer consisted of me asking god for self acceptance and for-giveness. Slowly my self esteem started to take form. I started to become confident in the woman I was becom-ing. I believed I needed to experience this type of pain in order to understand dealing with men on a deeper level. I now know that when a man's words and actions don't align I have to move on. I always felt I could change a man not necessarily with sex, but with my other character traits such as trust, faithfulness, and loyalty. That's just not the case with some men. I needed to experience this heartache in the form of a wake up call. I was always naïve and gullible and this was an example of one of those instances where I needed to trust my intuition more than ever and stop ignoring signs. I promised myself that I would never let anyone treat me as if I was wack ever again. I was smart, intelligent, beautiful, ambitious, and emotionally stable so why was I dealing with this kind of behavior. At the time I was in therapy working on becoming a better person when this experience happened to me. My therapist was the rock that I needed.

I thank God for my therapist Dr. Donnelly. Dr. Donnelly was heaven sent because he made me confront the little girl in my childhood who was always people pleasing and searching for love in the wrong places. During our sessions he reminded me of how far I've come and to stop comparing myself to others. I had to unlearn a lot of behaviors while working with him. Self doubt and low self worth weren't permissible in any of our therapy sessions. He made me confront my past head on and stop blaming myself for what people had done to me and the way they treated me. His therapy sessions taught me about having tunnel vision making sure my focus was always on myself and my goals. He reminded me of my beauty, intelligence, and my courage in overcoming so much up to this point. He allowed me to look at my situation differently and do the work on myself. His sessions were always beneficial because they made me look deep inward and get to the exact nature of my problem.

What I learned from my sessions with Dr. D was that I wanted to be loved in order to validate who I was. I used sex to chase love in hopes that it would not only validate me but that it would help me keep a man. I also realized that I was putting more focus on my biological clock rather than living life, not realizing there was more to life than worrying about if I would become a wife or mother and because my focus was in the wrong place every relationship suffered the same fate. In my mind I thought if I gave all of me to a man he would love me and see me for who I am, but because I was rushing these things, it gave birth to insecurities that I wasn't ready to confront. I was always treated like the faithful side piece because at some point I gave too much too soon and I'm honest enough to admit it. Men like Lawrence used my insecurities to their benefit. Dr. Donnelly always allowed me to feel what was going on with me internally and articulate it in order to understand exactly what I was feeling. In doing so I gained a new confidence in who I am. I thank Dr. Donnelly for being an amazing therapist. I attribute my new found confidence to his sessions; they truly helped to shape who I am today.

Those relationships I mentioned never lasted. It wasn't until I got wise enough to understand that dating is a process of elimination. It gives you insight on what you want and don't want and what you will tolerate and won't tolerate. I was never a serial dater. I was always searching for love with men who were incapable of loving me. It was in those sessions that I gained clarity into the issue I was having. Needless to say, I continued to do the work and search inward, which resulted in a lot of tears and prayers. I learned so much about myself in those sessions that I continued to hold my head high thanked Lawrence for the experience, and moved forward. I began to thrive again, and life looked promising.

I was finally getting over the heartbreak, and my heart was healing, business was thriving, and my edges were growing back. I was beginning to feel really great about myself when life knocked me down yet again. This time, I wasn't sure if I would be able to come back from this pain. I was experiencing a different kind of heartbreak all over again, and I wasn't sure if I would make it this time.

CHAPTER SIXTEEN

Brokenhearted

February 13th, 2011

My world as I knew it came crashing down. It was a Sunday afternoon around twelve thirty. I was on my way to see Dr. Donnelly, my therapist. I saw a few missed calls from my mother and something sank to the bottom pit of my stomach. She never calls me in repeated succession, as I dismissed the call, my phone continued to ring without ceasing. I look up and see it's my cousin Lachon calling me. I pulled over to take the call because at this point something tells me something is going on.

I answered the call and she's talking to me like normal, then she proceeds to ask me have I spoken to my father. I told her yes; that last Wednesday we spoke and told each other how much we loved and missed each other (he was on vacation in Jamaica).

She began to tell me there has been a terrible accident on the highway in Jamaica and that my dad had died as a result of that accident. Everything became a blur in that moment. I suddenly became dizzy; an instant headache permeated my skull. My palms began to sweat and the tears began to fall relentlessly. I hung up the phone on her, not aware of what I had just heard. I called my therapist, and he coached me through while I'm shaking, sweating, nauseated, dizzy and crying. My head felt like someone hit me with a hammer in my temple. It was as if I was in a terrible dream and had awakened distraught and out of sync with my body. I then called my girlfriend Khadijah bawling my eyes out. I couldn't move. My legs were shaking, nose running, head hurting and body was on fire. I stood on the side of the road for almost two hours crying. I knew I had to be strong for my mother and my family, but how? I needed to be strong for myself. I was weak both physically and mentally. I was still trying to process the information that was just delivered to me. I wanted to run away and crawl up under a rock. I didn't want to believe that my father my number one fan had died. I gathered myself off the side of the road and drove to my parent's house unaware of what awaits me.

My mother had fallen ill and was rushed to the hospital by the time I got to the house. She remained in the hospital for weeks. I cried for her because she had lost her one and only true love, she had lost the life she had come to know. How would she begin to pick up the pieces to move on? My mind was plagued with who, what, when, where, and why. How could God take my father away from us, this was one mistake he made that I couldn't come to peace with. I was mad at God for a very long time for taking my father. He took the only thing that meant the world to me. Apparently, my dad died as a result of a freak accident on the highway coming back from my uncle's funeral. Someone threw a boulder rock from the over pass and the rock landed in the car my dad was driving.

The heartbreak and pain of losing my father is something I still deal with until this day. My dad was my world. Despite all that we went through he never gave up on me and it was that unconditional love that kept me alive even in my addiction. The pain of losing a parent is inexplicable because in my mind I thought my parents were immortal and would live forever. That wasn't the case for my dad. I cursed God because I felt that he took the only man that ever loved me away from me. Right before his trip I remembered something he said to me that now serves as a comforting memory. He called me up a week before his trip and asked me to come over to go over his finances. He wanted to see how he could figure out a way to get money to bury his brother. So as we were figuring out ways to get the money. I was telling him some options available to him based on the budget we were working with. We were in his room talking and he said to me "I want you to know I love you very much, I'm proud of you and I cherish the ground you walk on" those words melted my heart and I told him I know you do and I love you too. I never knew that would be our last conversation.

I cursed God for months after my father's death and one day as I was praying my spirit became filled with forgiveness towards God. I stopped cursing him and I started thanking him for giving me the best dad ever. In that moment I forgave God and found comfort in knowing that I had a dad that went to war for me. He has kicked down doors to get me out of basements when I was getting high, he went on a war path determined to not let the streets get his daughter, although he was unsuccessful his love for me never waivered. He was always on the front lines fighting my battles for me. He never stopped praying for me. He loved me and let the world know that he loved me. Everyone that came into contact with my father loved him. He was real, genuine, funny and a man of his word.

It has been six years since his passing and although I miss him immensely I now know that the love he carried for me I now carry in my heart for him and others. My dad taught me character. He taught me that all I have in this world is my name and my word and that's what I stay true to. He was a provider, a husband, a father and a faithful man to my mother, and although he wasn't perfect he was my Dad and I loved the very ground he walked on. So after looking back over all that I knew my father to be, I began to speak to my mountains and thanking God for my dad. I began to look at things differently I would go to meetings and share my pain, cry, laugh, and be surrounded by love. I started praying for strength for me and my family and in time the pain subsided enough for me to keep moving forward.

I thank God for allowing my dad to see me clean and thriving. He was there for me when I bought my first house and had my house warming; all of my friends and coworkers loved my dad. He was such a genuine caring human being. I have so many funny memories of my father one in particular was when I got my first Bmw he felt like this was the crème de la crème of cars. He was with me at the dealership and he was more excited about the car than I was. He kept tooling around with all the features in the car and sticking his head out the sunroof. Everyone was laughing and having a good time. My dad was always the life of the party, he was always laughing and making sure everyone had a good time. These memories are what I take solace in, not his death, but his life and how he made people feel. I smile today and thank God for blessing me with the absolute perfect dad. I have no doubt in my heart that my dad would be proud and beaming with joy at the woman I am today.

CHAPTER SEVENTEEN

Tragedy After Tragedy

Our lives were turned upside down by the tragic circumstances that were overtaking my family, my auntie jess had suddenly passed away from cancer and in true succession my grandmother was next to pass away and my father's sister auntie celeste also passed away. I was hurting for my mother because everyone she loved was dying right before her eyes. The pain that sat behind her eyes told of her grief and fear as to whether she would be next. She was hurting and in pain and needed comfort. I was there every step of the way to speak life into her, to tell her I loved her and that I needed her. I was her therapist during those hard times. It was sad to see her lose everyone around her within less than a year, but she was clothed in strength and stayed in prayer. My mother had an air of equanimity that surrounded her while dealing with these unfortunate tragedies. I know this was nothing but the move of God covering and shielding her. I was in pure disbelief at how she handled herself during the roughest periods of her life. She never complained about how she felt, she just talked about how great her mother and sister was and how great God is. She found comfort in their memories and that's what kept her moving forward.

The loss of her husband and her mother is what really seemed to have shaken my mother's spirit the most. She hadn't quite heeled from the unexpected death of her husband and now her mother had falling ill to blood cancer and died unexpectedly. My grandmother was a woman that was centered and clothed in strength. She lived for God and did everything according to the move of her spirit. She came from a long lineage of strong women, who were matriarchs of their family. My grandmother's name was Winifred Mitchell, she was 5 five feet two inches tall and stout with beautiful caramel complected skin that sat behind round almond colored eyes, she had soft curly kinks sprinkled with wisdom of grays throughout her head. She was a gentle yet strong woman who had a peace about her that made anyone in her presence still. She gave the warmest hugs and the sweetest kisses and never raised her voice, but got her point across when she spoke. She was filled with so much knowledge and wisdom and when she spoke nothing but wisdom fell from her mouth and although I was too young to understand the wisdom she spoke of I now understand the things that she used to tell me in our conversations. She was my comfort, my seamstress, my cook, my prayer warrior and my world.

I loved visiting Canada in summers when I was younger because I would get to spend time with my grandmother who lived in Canada. Even though I knew she loved all her grandchildren equally, I always felt like I had a special place in her heart. Her voice was smooth like bourbon scotch and her heart was gentle, pure, and comforting. She was a Christian woman that never missed church on Saturdays. She had a church in Canada and one here in Perth Amboy.

What I loved about my grandmother is she taught all her children especially her girls how to be women and in turn these same lessons where taught to myself and my sister and my cousins. I loved to visit her because she would take great care of us. I miss my grandmother but she lived her life unapologetically and on her own terms, she was an amazing seamstress and made a living doing that in addition to being a world class hustler. She traveled up until her death. Jamaica was her home and no illness would stop her from traveling to her beloved home. Her sickness was quick and sudden she died from blood cancer. I loved everything about my grandmother, and losing her hurt equally as it did losing my dad.

I felt that God was punishing us. How could he allow us to hurt so much in the course of a year with repeated deaths? Our hearts were taking on copious amounts of pain in a short period of time and quite frankly I was tired of the pain of losing loved ones back to back. I understand that God doesn't make any mistakes, but I felt he was making a mistake with the death of my grandmother. She was the backbone of the family the matriarch and the thread that held the fabric of our family together. I know my mother misses her mother immensely, but we know she's in heaven resting in the care of God.

CHAPTER EIGHTEEN

Blessings in Disguise

One of the amazing blessings that came from the barrage of tragedies that were affecting us as a family was the opportunity and willingness to repair the relationship I never really had with my mother. My mother is an amazing woman that loves all her children equally, however I never felt a connection with my mother because I was closer to my dad, and I suspected she felt that my dad loved me more than he loved her, I felt there was always this air of competition and jealousy with her and I when it came to my father. That's all changed for the better but I can't help but to think about the hurt I felt growing up thinking that my mother never really cared about me because she saw me as a threat. That pain kept me stagnant in establishing a relationship with her when I was younger. I never had a mother daughter relationship with my mother. I couldn't go to her and talk to her about boys, my feelings, or anything that I was remotely interested in. I understand that culturally this is how some Caribbean women are with their children and I was no exception. She always felt like I loved my father more than her and that my father loved me more than he loved her I now know that's farthest from the truth but I can't help that I felt those emotions growing up.

My mother is a silent warrior, she's neither loud nor obnoxious, she's quiet and observant. She possesses the quiet strength of the proverbs 31 woman. I love the relationship we have today. I've learned my strength comes from her and my grandmother, she is kind, caring, and doesn't wear her disappointments on her sleeve. She's poised, calculating and stays strapped in the armor of

God. Our relationship is great today and I can attribute that to our love of God that brought us close even in tragedy. I can talk to her about everything and anything and she will give me truthful advice. She believes in me and loves every part of me. Even when she's struggling with something no one knows it. I love how she never wears her struggles for the world to see. She has taught me so much about who I am as a person flaws and all. These were all the blessings God gave me when I stopped looking at the problem and started focusing on rebuilding our relationship. Had my father not passed away I wouldn't have come to know the woman I call my mother. These were things that were blessings in disguise and for that I thank God

Another blessing that came out of this tragedy was the birth of my online and mobile business. These blessings fell into my lap during the worst time of my life. My father had just passed away and I was looking for ways to take my mind off his death while I was out of work. I began researching wholesale clothing retailers and researching how to start a business. It was my way of coping with his death. I had become numb and depressed and I found great joy in researching and shopping for clothes for my new business prospect. I already had a little style and flare with me, so I thought this would be a piece of cake to infuse my style/taste into the selection process of finding wholesale clothing suppliers that spoke to my style aesthetic.

I had an eye for fashion and quickly started buying pieces that were unique, made of good quality and affordable for my customers. I started going to apparel trade shows and scouring magazines for the latest trends in fashion. It became second nature for me. I hustled in this business and met some nice and not so nice people. The name sense of style boutique came to me in my sleep, and the thought process behind this name would mean a change in your style once you left our business you would now have a sense of style. It was cheesy but it worked for me. I began to focus on this new venture and surprisingly it took off. I started selling clothes out of my car, taking them to work and selling them to the ladies on my job, going to salons, and vending everywhere. Within six months I opened my first storefront.

In October of 2011 I opened up my first brick and mortar storefront in Linden, NJ. It was an insightful experience that I wasn't prepared for. One of the few reasons was the location. I was on a one way street with little to no parking, secondly the population in that area was predominantly Polish and lastly I had no clue about running a business so it was very hard to make a profit with these factors. I was determined to make it work, I promoted my store on all social media platforms, in local ads, and word of mouth, yet I still wasn't prepared because I was running the store part time and working around the clock fulltime. With the store came great responsibilities it became very hard for me to pay my mortgage and overhead charges associated with the store. I had to work long hours doing a lot of overtime just to pay the overhead charges, utility bills, and my employee it became cumbersome to say the least. That was a very challenging year for me. After a year I decided to close down and reroute my business online so I opened up www.sosboutique.net online. This was easier and less tedious; thankfully the site is still fully operational. In addition to the website in 2015 we launched our first mobile fashion truck which is pretty much a store on wheels. This allowed me to offer door to door services to my clients as well as vend at festivals and corporate events.

The boutique introduced me to so many amazing women that I now call my friends. I was able to build my relationships with these women who support everything that I do, and I in turn I support them in whatever their endeavors are. I'm thankful for a lot of the blessings that were bestowed upon me once I became clean. A lot of things haven't been easy for me while still in business and I understand that to whom much is given much is required. There were days when running the business became a hindrance for me. I wanted to give up, but my pride wouldn't allow me to. I told myself I'd rather fail forward than quit. I was able to recognize these blessings because of my willingness to become God centered and invite him into all my affairs. These blessings that were birthed out of tragedies have allowed me to truly become who I envisioned I'd become and for that im truly thankful to God.

CHAPTER NINETEEN

A Different Kind of Love

In 2012 I was single and not looking to meet anyone because lets face it my selection in men was the absolute worst and quite honestly I was learning to love all of me flaws and all. Let's keep in mind that a few months prior I was nursing a broken heart from dealing with Lawrence, so love wasn't exactly something I was looking for. One Saturday afternoon in April I was on the phone with my girlfriend Cynthia talking about that evening's activity. Apparently there was a party in my area that she was going to. I told her I would go, but I really had no intentions of going. Later on that evening I was asleep in bed and she kept blowing up my phone, reluctantly I got up got dressed and decided to hang out for a little. We were headed to some new club in downtown New Brunswick called Pearl. I met Robert on this very night on April 14th 2012 while fighting for a parking spot in New Brunswick on the corner of Paterson and Spring Street.

I pulled up to the parking space as one of his co workers was either coming or going, so I pulled over and asked him was the spot taken, Robert then replied to me the only way he would give me the spot is unless I gave him my number. I thought to myself this will go no where. I had no plans for this guy whatsoever, he was nerdy, short, wore glasses and just seemed corny to me. He simply was not my cup of tea. I liked reformed bad boys with a little street edge and he seemed like he liked to read the newspaper with his legs crossed, not that there's anything wrong with reading the newspaper with your legs crossed, that just wasn't what I was used to. I wanted someone that I could relate to, that understood my struggles and where I came from. We exchanged numbers so I could get the parking space and went on our way. The next day he called me we spoke for a while on the phone and surprisingly it was a refreshing conversation. I learned a lot about him in the first few conversations which made me excited about going out on a date with him.

A week later we had our first date at a sushi spot in the area. We talked about a lot of different things on our first date including family, career, life, news and views on various topics. From that night forward I was sold on this nerdy reformed bad boy with a lot of street edge. He lived down the street from me. So we connected more and went out on dates every weekend. He was reserved, mindful, fiscally responsible, smart, handsome, and like to drink coffee and read the newspaper with his legs crossed (lol). He taught me a lot about my self in ways I didn't know existed. I was always impulsive and reacted emotionally. He taught me to think things through first before I reacted and be a little bit more calculating about how I approached things in my life. He made me look at things from a different angle in addition to helping me put a budget in place. This was the first guy that went over a budget with me. He was always there to lend moral support and help me pay attention to matters that concerned my business and my personal well being.

When I met Rob I was my complete authentic self I was no longer trying to fit into anyone's idea of who I should be. We complimented each other very well and I fell in love with him. I wanted everything with him. He completely saw me in my raw element. When I had nothing whatsoever he never left my side. He was there for me, and although our relationship didn't have an official label his actions led me to believe we were dating exclusively and I was ok with it.

Eight months into my new relationship with Robert I lost my job of 9 years. I was shocked at the chain of events that was happening to me in the blink of an eye.

During my addiction I had wrecked a lot of havoc on my employer and subsequently I was put on discipline after discipline. Those disciplines were a culmination of all those years that I didn't come to work or messed up on accounts or had customer complaints. These myriad of disciplines were a calculating factor in my termination. Another aggregating factor in my termination was an argument I had with a co worker that lead the company to believe that I was creating an extremely hostile work environment. In addition to those ostensible factors they also ran reports that purported that I was misusing company property and time.

December 11, 2012

I was brought into the front office with the manager's of my department, one of those manager's happened to be the supervisor that I had gotten into an argument with a few years back, he had now moved up into upper management. Of course I felt that this was his personal jab against me. I was fired that day for the things I mentioned earlier. I gathered my things and I got in my car and did two things I cried my eyes out and started praying to God to guide me through this storm. In that instant a peace that surpasses my understanding came over me and I felt a calmness come over me that reassured me that I would be alright. It was as if God was holding me in his arms. I didn't know what was happening to me at this time I just knew I was scared and all I could think about was my bills, my mortgage, and my financial stability.

On my drive home I called my mother and told her I was fired form my job and she offered to help me if I needed it. I then proceeded to call Robert he was very supportive and kind. He offered advice as to how we would get through this storm together and not to focus on it just get some rest. I was afraid of the unknown but God showed up for me in major ways. I went through the emotions of grieving the loss of my job. I cried, I got angry, and I stayed in bed for a few days. After about three days in bed I finally got up out of the funk and started to proactively secure my future. I perused the internet looking for Jobs, I called my mortgage company and told them I had loss my job and they offered me some numbers to contact the state regarding programs to help me with my mortgage.

One of those programs was a little unknown program funded by the government called the NJ Home keepers Program. It helped pay your mortgage and keep you in your home. I applied for the program online. A few months went by and I hadn't heard from anyone. I contacted the state and they gave me the number to my housing counselor. It seems as though they had dropped the ball and forget to process my application, which automatically gave me an edge up against anyone else. They were afraid I would report them to the state which I didn't intend to but I pretended as if I would. They pulled my application brought me in for debt counseling and processed my application.

CHAPTER TWENTY

Weathering the Storm

A few weeks later I'm out and about running some errands and I received an email from the housing and mortgage finance agency here in Trenton, NJ telling me that I was approved for the grant to help me pay my mortgage. I immediately pulled over into the rite aide parking lot. I combed through the email word for word; I began to praise and worship God with tears streaming down my face. I began to minister to him how thankful I was for all that he was doing for me. This was a huge blessing for me considering that I was running low on funds and knew that I wouldn't have been able to pay my mortgage if I didn't get this grant. I was so thankful for what he was doing I cried out to him thanking him for blessing me and making a way for me. That day I felt a glimmer of hope in my situation and I knew for sure that God was riding shotgun with me.

I began the process of allocating my retirement funds into an IRA and mutual funds to hold me over until I found another job. I applied for unemployment and even attempted to apply for public assistance. I was denied public assistance because I made too much (go figure). I collected unemployment for one month and found a job making significantly less than what I was making at my previous job. I was making eighteen dollars an hour and I was content. I learned to budget my money and I was honestly at peace. I began working for a pharmaceutical company in their maintenance department in February of 2013. I was going through a purge in my life a lot of people that I worked with and hung out with were being removed from my life and I couldn't have been more pleased. There was a reason God removed me from my previous employer because I was caught up in the wrong things at work. I was gossiping, fighting with people, and just not being my best self. I never suspected I would be fired but when it happened I trusted God in everything, and although I struggled I understood that the valley I was in wouldn't last forever. I know he was separating me from people that I had asked him to remove out my life and I couldn't be more than happy. I was going through a period of being uncomfortable in order to be able to trust God wholeheartedly. Oftentimes we ask God to do some things in our lives and then we get upset when He actually does it in his timing and not our timing.

While on hiatus from my employer I learned a lot about life. I learned that I was crippled by fear and money at my previous job. That alone kept me stagnant in my thinking and fully reliant on my job. This period was marred with test and trials that made me strong and resilient. Nothing but rejection after rejection filled my inboxes and voicemails from potential employers. I was forced to Budget my money and stop spending frivolously, I went from making over a hundred thousand dollars a year to barely making less than forty thousand dollars a year for 2 years and I not only survived, but I saved money and was at peace. It was in that moment that I knew that God was with me and never left my side.

I was cognizant of God's presence, power, and anointing over my life; he kept me in perfect peace while fighting the battles ahead of me. I knew for a fact that with all that I was going through that my trust and faith in God would never be nebulous. This is when I prayed more, went to church more, and stayed in the word more. I believed and operated in faith and relied on his every word. I joined my church and was front row every Sunday. My life and future began to take shape. I was at peace, something I never experienced before. I began to trust in God's word and being obedient. From time to time I would spice up my resume and went on few interviews only to be rejected repeatedly. I couldn't get a job to save my life, and that's because God was ordering my steps and I needed to be still and trust in him.

During that time my union had contacted me and told me they wanted to arbitrate the case, because they felt I was fired without just cause and the firing was an act of retaliation. I gave them the okay to fight the case, hey what could I lose. I knew I wasn't this bad person they made me out to be so I wanted them to fight for me because in my heart I knew I didn't do those things they accused me of. I kept my faith and lived my life. In those two years I traveled and enjoyed life. I grew closer to Robert and I felt something real and tangible with him albeit we weren't in a relationship his presence in my life was comforting and I grew to fall in love with him.

As I continued to hustle doing vending gigs, I would oftentimes pray and cry because I was broke. My prayers became pleas of desperation. I was struggling to make ends meet and my assignment with the temp agency was coming to a close. A few weeks later I started working at another company for a few months making a little more than the previous temp job but less than I made at my previous job. I kept grinding and as life is happening I get a call from my union telling me they scheduled a hearing for my arbitration case. I had forgotten all about my union since I hadn't heard from them in months. The news about my arbitration made me happy yet scared so I got on my knees and I prayed and asked God to enter into the situation and if it was in his will let his will be done.

As I prepared for my arbitration case in late July 2014 I was nervous because I didn't know what to expect, I had grown so much in Christ that even though my faith was strong I was nervous and happy to tell my truth. We met for the arbitration in an office park in Somerset NJ. The arbitration took place in a big conference room with a large table and chairs. The court appointed reporter was there to record the arbitration hearing. My supervisor at the time of my termination was there along with the manager that terminated me and a few managers from human resources and industrial relations, as well as the arbitrator. The attorney representing the company was relentless in her pursuit to paint this picture of me being a bad employee, I mean I will say that my reputation at the company wasn't the best, I was considered loud, outspoken, arrogant, and challenging at best, but once I got clean I worked to clean my image up. I didn't do anything out of the scope of my job, so to hear her speak of my character in such a way automatically had me on the defense.

I was told by my union lawyers that this is to be expected and that I was to keep my composure. The attorney rambled on about my work performance and why the company was justified in firing me, then they called my supervisor at the time of my termination to the stand and asked him questions about my productivity and of course they coached him to lie and he did that very well. They also spoke of my disciplines and how they believed I took advantage of the system. The situation did not look promising for me. I started to lose my faith and counted myself out.

The attorney representing the company finally wrapped up her closing statement stating that they have provided more than enough evidence as to why I should not get my job back and they were more than confident that I would not get my job back. I must be honest my chances looked slim to none after they wrapped up everything. We finally broke for lunch and I went to the bathroom and I prayed to God that if it was in his will to allow me to tell my truth and be as honest, transparent, and forthcoming as I can be.

After lunch arbitration was resumed and I was called to the stand. I got on the stand and they asked me questions pertaining to my employment such as how long I worked there, what was my role at the company, what did my average work day consist of, and things of that nature. My productivity was called into question based on their statistical reports that were based on an 8 hour work day; I explained in great detail the role of my job and that those statistics weren't accurate because I worked twelve to fourteen hours daily on overtime. I spoke about my stats and how they didn't correlate to my 14 hour shift. I explained in detail the nature of a call center environment and how it operates from a service representative point of view. I spoke about the lack of resources that were readily available to me and other representatives, in terms of resolving customer issues. Not having those resources was a contributing factor in why I had such high loss time in certain areas of the productivity report in question. I also spoke about how the company had changed over to a new software system and had a lot of internal problems with this new system, which also contributed to my productivity not being status quo. They called into question the reports they ran that I was never made aware of. I explained to the arbitrator that these reports were never brought to my attention during our one on one sessions with my supervisor in fact I was showing signs of improvement in the areas that needed improvement, not to mention that my supervisor was new to the position and was always in supervisory training so the disconnect between him and the team was evident. We didn't have an immediate supervisor to report to in his absence. I spoke my truth about every question that was presented to me.

All I ever wanted was the truth to be told. As we wrapped up the arbitration I wasn't sure which direction it would go in favor of, but I was just happy to tell my truth about what I felt was an unjust termination. My executive union counsel told me that I did great on the stand. I was poised, articulate, and had a clear and concise recollection of the chain of events that happened two years prior. He then proceeded to tell me that it would take about 8 weeks to hear anything back pertaining to the case. It would be around September 6th when the arbitrator would have a ruling. I went home said a prayer, fasted, and meditated on God's words. I left it alone and told God if it's in his will let your will be done. I went on with my life as usual. I was back to hustling my clothes out my car and working and loving on Rob.

CHAPTER TWENTY-ONE

Back Like I never Left

September 6th, 2014

I received a call from my executive board union president, I searched his voice for clues as to whether or not I won the case, he began the conversation in a very monotone voice. I again began to search his voice for clues that would give me any indication as to how the conversation would go. He began by stating that never in the history of his appointment as the executive board president has he ever seen a case of this magnitude. He then proceeded to tell me that the union tried their best and didn't know which way the arbitrator would rule, just as he said that I said thank you Noah for all that you've done for me I know it was a long run but we did the best we could, he stopped me in my tracks and said we won. I dropped the phone and fell to my knees and began praying and thanking God. Tears streamed down my face as I started to praise and worship god. Thanking him for being a faithful god. I had fasted for a week and sacrificed some things as an offering to God and he gave me my job back. All my struggling wasn't in vain.

As I came to I could hear Noah yelling into the phone I picked up the phone and he said I'm not done yet. He said not only did you get your job back, but the company has to pay you back all your back pay from the day you were terminated up until the day you returned to work which would be on September 22, 2014. Not only did the arbitrator rule in my favor he also ruled that I get all my back pay. I thanked Noah and we went over some details about my start date and hung up the phone.

I cried, prayed, and worshipped God for an hour straight. I called Robert with the good news. That was the best news I ever received in my life he was so excited for me and told me he was happy for me. He had seen me struggle for over two years and now things were turning around in my favor.

I arrived at work on September 22, 2014. I was excited to be back at work. My mindset was different and I was met with congratulations and welcome backs. My immediate supervisor met with me and we went over some objectives. For a few months I sat and listened to calls until I went back to training. I wasn't the same in terms of the person I was when I was terminated. I no longer entertained certain people or office gossip. My experience had taught me to focus on God and myself and no one else. Today I thrive in my position and I focus on the many projects I'm currently working on and stay clear of trouble.

CHAPTER TWENTY-TWO

Change is Imminent

Robert and I were dating for close to four years before things started to unravel. Things began to take a turn for the worst so to speak, because I was at a point where I no longer wanted to be friends with benefits. I wanted to have the security of a man in my life. He had been around me for close to four years so at that point he knew whether this is something he wanted long term with me or not, but he could never be honest with me, so he continued to string me along with empty promises. We had plenty of conversations in respect to where the relationship was going, his response was usually the same "we were friends and he doesn't want to have any labels" I like you and its working for both us, as long as you're happy". This is was what he would tell me, I respected it and still stayed. His actions were in line with how he felt about me, whenever I needed him he was there for me no matter what. I really felt like we were in an exclusive relationship based on his actions and the things he would tell me. Our situation ship was convenient for both of us because I was focusing on other projects and didn't require much from him, just to be there when I needed him, which he was. I was self sufficient, stable, and mentally focused on work and my personal development. Rob and I spoke about everything nothing was off limit. Every time I made attempts to leave he held me hostage mentally.

The relationship was a big contradiction in my eyes at this point. Plenty of times I poured my soul out to him and it was like it went through one ear and out the other. Every time I tried to move on it was hard for me, because he was always in the picture calling, texting, coming by and acting as if nothing was wrong. I wanted to move on, but I was too vested in what we had to move on. I do take total responsibility for the part I played in the situation; I was given plenty of signs that I ignored. I ignored my intuition and subsequently lost my credibility. This is important for me to acknowledge and address because I knew better but I let my guard down and grew complacent. I used him as a crutch for my own emotional reasons. In my crazy thinking I felt it was better to have a piece of something with someone as opposed to having nothing and dealing with the dating pool.

Although I accept and take responsibility for the part I played in the situation playing out for as long as it did, I refuse to pretend that he didn't help to perpetuate the madness. I felt like I was deserving of a good solid relationship I had proven my loyalty to him. We both continued to perpetuate the illusion that we were content with each other until he revealed himself for who he really was.

CHAPTER TWENTY-THREE

Bruised but Not Broken

October 29th 2016

My perfect little world was once again shaken up as I was rocked hard with the revelation that the man I had grown to love and been intimate with for years was now a married man. The revelation slapped the Jesus out of me. I had just gotten in from styling a client for a photo shoot. I had taken a shower and was relaxing in bed. I was tooling around with Facebook and it was as if the Holy Spirit told me to go onto to snap chat. I went onto snap chat and the first story uploaded was Rob's cousin's story. For some odd reason I clicked on the story and there I see Rob in a suit walking hand in hand with his bride through what seems to be a park with fully bloomed autumn leaves and beautiful trees. The next story is of them at the reception and she is draped in traditional African Wedding Attire and they are dancing and enjoying themselves. I watched that video 52 times and what I gathered from the background was that this was a carefully planned well executed wedding that included beautiful floral arrangements beautiful bridesmaids and tons of planning and prepping.

My heart broke all over again, because in that moment I felt she had stolen my happily ever after. I was broken, hurt, angry, vengeful, and disappointed all at once. How did I not see the signs? How could I have been sleeping with an engaged to be married man? Why did he lie to me and tell me he was going to visit his dad in Florida? So many questions entered my mind who, what, when, where, why. How could I have been this naïve yet again?

I couldn't contain my tears as they fell like streams of river from my eyes. I called up my girlfriend Qiana to tell her what I saw and of course Qiana being the ever so positive person says to me your imagining things that's not Rob, it can't be he's in Florida. I'm crying and telling her I know what the hell this man look like. I had been sleeping with him for four plus years. I know his awkward poses, dances, and facial moves. I jumped in my car and headed to her house to show her this video that I had just seen. She and her husband looked at the video and determined that the man in the video was Rob.

The pain my heart felt was a pain I wouldn't wish on anyone. It was the pain of disappointment more than anger, I called Rob's friend Danny and asked him did Rob get married he answered me assuredly with conviction in his voice that yes he did. He began to tell me that he was supposed to be apart of the wedding, but he couldn't make it for whatever reason, I hung up the call with him and just fell into Qiana's arm. All she could say was that she was so sorry, and so was I. I was sorry for doing this to myself again; sorry for putting myself through this pain again, sorry for not putting myself first, sorry for the fear of being alone, I was just a sorry ass at this time. Had I followed and listened to my instinct I wouldn't be in this pain yet again. Did I really have a right to complain though? The relationship had ran its course, and we were going through the motions. The hurt I felt was mostly the feeling of being used, rejected, and discarded.

This was the same man that told me he didn't want children and doesn't see himself married, and now he was married and supposedly expecting a child with someone else. In that moment everything I had hoped and prayed for had dissolved right before my eyes. How could I have not picked up on the signs, was I that naïve or was my focus in the wrong place? These were questions that played out in my mind. I didn't have a choice in the matter, simply because I didn't know who I was dealing with or that I was sleeping with an engaged to be married man. I felt like my choice was taken away from me. Had he told me I would have left no matter how much pain I was in.

After a few days and some self reflection I stopped blaming myself and realized that the man I thought I knew was someone who lacked any kind of character no matter his age. I then realized the reason why I had been so hurt was because he was emotionally manipulative to me and I used him as an emotional crutch. As long as he satisfied my emotional needs I was ok with being com-placent. I began to search inwards as I always do when I encounter any disruption in my life. The devil wanted me to blame myself, but the God I serve wouldn't allow me to simply because this had nothing to do with me and more so to do with who this person was. I understand that this had to happen in that season to push me forward into my purpose.

I also realized in that moment that my strength was being tested. I didn't eat or sleep for a few days, Within 24 hours I found his new wife and her entire family on Facebook and because I wanted him to feel my pain, I sent his wife a long lengthy message with pictures attached detailing our relationship. I then proceeded to block everyone. She never responded, but I later learned she saw the messages. That night I asked God to forgive me for sending the message, the rational part of me wanted to take the Christian route and leave it alone, but the emotionally hurt part of me wanted him to feel the same pain I was feeling. The devil was so busy at this time, because he was feeding me with negativity about who I was.

My thoughts were filled with being unworthy, rejected, disrespected, and not good enough. I knew that to be farthest from the truth, but somehow I began to entertain the thoughts. I was having a pity party for myself. I was mourning the loss of my homie, lover, and friend. I invested so much time and to see the man I loved married to someone else pierced my heart like a knife. I had shared so much with this man. My hopes, fears, and dreams. To see those very same things given to someone else hurt my very existence. I was intimate with this man a week before his wedding. This was the man I spent Christmas's and summer vacations with. What was happening? This had to be a sick nightmare I was experiencing. No way was rob married. The last time we were intimate was a week before his wedding. We went on a date talked and enjoyed each other's company which was of course pretty routine for us. He told me he was going to his father's house in Florida to visit him and watch the Jacksonville and Panthers football game. To find out he actually went to partake in his marriage to someone else was a shock to my system.

I knew at some point throughout our friendship Robert cared about me and loved me because he told me, but he was never fully committed or able to show that to me, now years later he is married to someone else and moving on as if him and I had nothing. What that indicates to me is that he lacked good moral character and he is a coward. I realized quickly that he lacked any moral compass and was missing a sensitivity chip. The fact that I never had any clue or inclination that Rob was engaged to be married made me more upset because he took my choice away from me. As I mentioned beforehand if he had told me he was engaged to be married I would have been hurt yes, but I would have respected his decision and moved on with my life, and that's what hurts the most.

At one point I felt like I was a prop in his sick twisted game. I thank god for being instrumental in my life because I honestly can say that if I didn't have God in my life I would probably end up back in jail. I am also very thankful I no longer suffer from low self esteem and understand that rejection is a part of life, because if I wasn't emotionally stable I don't trust that I wouldn't have been in another orange jumpsuit. I suddenly now understood how some women can lose their mind and freedom behind a man. I'm moving through this pain sober and clean. I'm learning a lot about myself in terms of my tolerance for certain things and picking up on the signs early enough.

God sent me so many signs with Robert and I ignored every last one of them all while praying to him to make this relationship work. It was never supposed to be long term as I look back over the relationship. I placed a lot of blame on myself for using that man as a crutch for my emotional needs, which was due in part because I didn't want to jump back into the dating pool, when all the signs indicated that I needed to dive back in. I thank God for how he allowed this chapter to close out for without him I would have still continued to want more from someone who wasn't willing to give me more. Looking back over this experience this guy was a sociopath and a master manipulator and I'm very thankful this chapter of my life is over.

CHAPTER TWENTY-FOUR

Preparing Me for My Purpose

A few months have elapsed and looking back I'm thankful to God that I dodged a bullet. He showed me so many signs and I ignored them hoping that through prayer, sacrifice, and supplication the man I once loved would change. What I now realize is he wasn't designed for me and I've come to terms with that today. What hurt the most were all the things I wanted with him that he was incapable of giving me. The man that I had loved at one point was incapable of loving me because he was a broken man that didn't love himself. This man was an opportunist that took advantage of women. He never knew what love looked or felt like so his idea and interpretation of love was misconstrued and misguided at best. He preyed on women that were vulnerable and looking for love such as myself.

Although I was hurting I never once held any malice in my heart nor was I vengeful. I just prayed to God for strength to help me get through this rough patch. Although my ego was bruised it wasn't broken and I refused to operate as if I was broken.

I've since forgiven him, because I forgave myself first. I forgave myself for being a hopeless romantic who wanted something from a man that was incapable of giving me anything more than sex. I forgave myself for falling for potential instead of reality, I forgave myself for losing myself in lust hoping it would turn to love, I forgave myself for seeing the best in him but getting the worse he had to offer in return, I forgave myself for wanting a future with someone who didn't see me in theirs. I forgave myself for believing the lies, I for-gave myself for ignoring all the signs God had shown me, I forgave myself for not being strong enough to let go when I needed to, I forgave myself because I have grown and learned from this experience. I'm ready to move forward in my life unapologetically with my head held high. Once I forgave those parts of me the work came easy. I realized that this man's happiness wasn't tied to my destiny. How could I be hateful to someone who purportedly found happiness, everyone deserves happiness and if he found that happiness with someone else then that was his destiny. Once I began to think in this context the healing came sooner than later. I washed my hands of the situation and move forward in who God said I was and never looked back.

The work came after I forgave myself for the things I learned during our time together which were things I jot-ted down and threatened to never repeat such as: enter-ing into any situations that rendered being friends with benefits, giving too much of myself too fast, ignoring the signs, identifying emotionally manipulative behaviors and lastly thinking I can change how he feels about me if I did this or that. I now understand that when a man tells you he's just looking to be friends. He's really telling you he doesn't want anything more than that with you. He will not take the time to invest in you. He will feed you breadcrumbs for as long as you allow him to. A man knows what he wants period.

Once I learned the lesson from my past experiences I took a different approach to dating. I began dating as if I already had a child. Would this man be a good provider, father figure, and protector? Is he family oriented, does he serve his community, is he physically, emotionally, and financially healthy. Does he love God like I do? What are his core values and do they align with mine? Once I began applying those questions to potential suitors they all started to drop like flies. I took it a step further and invited God into my love life and asked him to prepare me to be a wife and select my husband for me. I stopped looking, searching, wanting, and hoping. I've come to terms with being happily single.

One thing I've learned from going through this experience yet again is that I need to continue to work on forgiving myself and surround myself with my village of prayer warriors. Now more than ever is a crucial time for me. My growth although contingent upon the experiences I have gone through isn't confined to just this experience alone but a culmination of everything that has gotten me to this point. How I react and handle situations should be based on experience and wisdom rather than emotions. In knowing this I began to reach out to people who I knew would pray incessantly on my behalf.

I encountered so many people that kept telling me the same thing repeatedly and treating me as if I didn't have feelings. That bothered me because some people treated me more like a martyr than a human being with feelings and I understand from their perspective why they would treat me like that. They had seen me overcome obstacles after obstacles so it was expected for them to treat me in that manner. However, I was hurting and everyone told me the same thing you're amazing, beautiful, and strong you'll bounce back. I didn't want to be seen as those adjectives. I just wanted to be human and feel what I was feeling. I wanted to cry, talk, scream and laugh but it's as if I wasn't supposed to feel these things because I was strong. I hated that strong woman complex; because it leaves such a negative connotation. Strong women hurt too, I just wanted a hug and to be told it's ok to feel the way I felt, not to be made to feel dismissive because I was strong and I would more than likely get over it. I stopped sharing my feelings and retreated back into the care of God.

I began reading the word everyday sometimes two times a day because I needed to talk to God, I wanted to protect my spirit and energy and I was afraid of my own thoughts. So I prayed more fervently for strength every single morning, afternoon, and night. I was more focused on putting my energy where it belong which was in Christ. I joined bible study classes and became active in my church. I was determined not to become bitter, vengeful or hateful. Instead I turned inwards and started to look at the situation from an introspective perspective. I began to speak positivity over my life with positive affirmations daily, repeating that this wasn't about me but more about that person, focusing on writing this book, and starting my new business. Before I knew it my heart began to heal, I started to feel good about myself again, and my smile was brighter than ever.

Let me be a little more clairvoyant as to why I approached and centered my thinking around God and his word. I have a disease better known as the disease of addiction this disease is centered in my thinking and feelings. It preys on my psyche and tells me I don't have a disease and that I'm fine. I have to be mindful in my thinking if not there's the propensity that I could quite possible relapse. With that in mind I try to be in tune with what and how I'm feeling. I focus on what I am feeding and telling myself mentally? If I'm not careful it will tell me I'm the reason why this is happening to me. It always serves to remind me of my pass and why I'm not deserving of certain blessings in my life. Knowing how my disease operates I have to be proactive in putting my focus and energy on God and his word because it's the only weapon I have to fight my disease of addiction. This is what works for me and has kept me clean for 9 years.

What I learned through my experience with these significant relationships is that I attracted master manipulators who at times had me questioning my integrity and self worth. My feelings were always subtly dismissed or reduced to that of nothing. I was always made to think I was doing something wrong or left feeling confused and crazy when dealing with these men. The warning signs in these relationships were very subtle and if I wasn't careful I would miss the signs. Understanding where the root cause of the issues came from I was left with a few questions that I needed to answer truthfully to make sure the pattern wasn't repeated again.

I wrote three questions down that I wanted to explore more in depth: 1) why do I attract the same types of men? 2) Why do I make myself readily available so soon? 3) Do I believe that being in a relationship will complete me? I sought to break down each question and answer them as truthfully as possible in an effort to heal completely. Question number 1 was easy for me to answer because I knew I attracted men who were less than me who can learn from me and I can build into the ideal mate that I wanted. Seeing that I was always looking to help and build people, I took on these men as if they were my personal projects. If they could see that I'm great at taking care of their needs while maintaining my independence they would see that I was loyal, faithful, and worth it and they would be readily available to commit to me.

When it came to the conversation of commitment these men put up resistance wherever possible. I now understand there wasn't a need for them to commit to me because I didn't give them a chance to prove to me if they were worthy of me. It was vice versa. This has always been an issue as I was always trying to prove myself to people because I wanted to fit in and be well received which is rooted in people pleasing since early childhood. I also did this in relationships with these men.

Another pattern I noticed was that I attracted men who were still in love with their mother meaning that every woman had to measure up to their mother. They never fully detached themselves from their mother's breast. They were emotionally vacant and spoiled and couldn't really navigate the world without the help of their mother's, who were readily there to pick up the mess they made. Knowing that I was able to spot these issues in these men I was too afraid to say anything or voice my opinion in fear that they wouldn't like me or they would think I'm too strong willed. I now know that I gravitated to men who were incapable of loving me the way I knew I needed to be loved, but I wanted to undertake them as projects to mold them into the men I wanted them to be in order to love me the way I knew I needed to be loved these projects failed miserably.

In response to question two, I made myself readily available to these men to prove to them that I was a prized possession. I was faithful, loyal, and gave them the benefit of the doubt. I was more invested in making sure they saw me fit to be their girlfriend and ultimately wife material. My insecurities and low self worth screamed loudly that I was better suited for the role of a side chick. I gave too much of myself very early into meeting these men. I presented my resume to them in a beautifully crafted empty gift box. I wore my accomplishments on my sleeve and my independence like my favorite silk blouse in hopes that they would see me for the beautiful women that I was. I would pour into them my time and resources (not money) all while ignoring my intuition because I was determined to find love. This was the worst thing I could have ever done to my self esteem. These men used me and treated me like the old faithful chick that I was without putting any real effort into really getting to know me. I was too busy trying to fulfill their fantasy and my destiny without consulting with God. I felt if I had the perfect job, the perfect degree, the perfect relationship, the perfect life that I would be complete. That couldn't be farthest from the truth because every where I went there was Melissa.

I realized that in order for me to be complete I had to be completely happy with who I was, and I can't say I was happy with myself for a very long time. I looked for outside influences to fill the void of happiness. it started at a very young age searching for happiness. I searched through people, places, and things and always ended up empty handed. It wasn't until I went through all that I went through to realize that only I could make myself happy. I had to learn to fall completely in love with myself the good and the bad. Happiness for me is a choice and everyday I choose to make myself happy no matter what I'm going through. I positively affirm to the universe that I am deserving of everything I desire. My choices are now reflected and rooted in my happiness.

For a very long time I measured happiness to things and people. I wanted the perfect relationship but had no clue what the perfect relationship was or anyone to model it after. I was also dealing with liking Melissa who at the time was insecure and struggling with issues of low self esteem and valuation. These men were able to pick up on that quickly and used it to their advantage to spoon feed me just enough fluff for me to think it was something special we had. I was never one to subscribe to the notion of loving someone and not expecting to be loved in return. We're humans its part of the law of reciprocity, I want to know that there's a feeling of mutuality on both ends. I expected to be loved in return, but that's not how love works. These examples of love made me understand that this wasn't the type of love I wanted. I knew that love wasn't supposed to leave me feeling bitter, sad, and confused. It was important for me to take a step back and assess my life from a different angle.

Experience is the best teacher and I'm thankful to the men that helped me to get a better understanding on the nature of relationships and what I have to offer. I'm fully aware of who I am today. Those experiences showed me exactly what I didn't want and made me deserving of the love that is yet to come. I no longer entertain anything or anyone that will have me questioning my self worth or who I am as a person. Although I loved these men I now understand that my interpretation of love was skewed. I created a fairytale in my head as to what I believed love was supposed to be and thought I could play it out in real life.

CHAPTER TWENTY-FIVE

Purposed Through Pain

Everything that has happened in my life has been done according to the plan and will of God, I started thinking retrospectively about my life and how far I had come. I knew I was being shifted into something greater than I could ever imagine. I had forgiven myself for the way I treated myself, for doubting myself when I knew I deserved better but couldn't see my way to better. I have to say today I'm so much wiser and smarter in how I treat myself. It's funny how we have to allow others to treat us like crap in order to teach ourselves how we are to be treated. How we treat ourselves sets the tone for how others will treat us. I began journaling my thoughts again. although I had been writing for well over 3 years I never felt that I had anything to say so I would journal a little and put it down, but I knew somehow a book was inside of me and it was during those introspective moments I heard God tell me he will help me with my book. I prayed to him and asked him to help me to be completely honest, transparent, and have the willingness to put everything on the front line based on my interpretation and perception of the situations I went through.

Everything I went through has qualified me to help someone else who's dealing with obstacles and don't know how to grow through them. I decided that I would use this book as a catalyst to help me touch lives and empower women. This isn't about me and that's why I had no problem sharing my experience, strength, and hope to help others. This opportunity is for me to share, inspire, encourage, and motivate women. I decided I wanted my legacy to be rooted in service something that

I'm passionate about. I always found joy in helping others so why not start where I am and focus more on being of service. I am a firm believer that God and the Universe will reward your benefits as long as your intentions are pure and done with a good heart.

I'm thankful to God for allowing me to go through my valleys unscathed and although I don't look like the hell I been through, just know that I'm not exempt from hurt, pain, tragedy, and anything that life decides to throw at me, it's how I choose to handle life lessons that determines the outcome that I'm seeking. When you've lived such a negative life like I have for so long you become consumed with negativity. I had to unlearn all my negative behaviors and thinking. My mindset slowly began to change once I developed a relationship with God. My prayers consisted of him transforming my mindset and self-acceptance. I began to notice the miracles and favors he was blessing me with. I now became reliant on my faith and trust in him. I knew these miracles and favors were due in part to me being obedient but also because I began to think and expect positive changes in my life. I began looking at things from a positive perspective and doing the work. Prayer, faith, and hard work is how I became successful in thinking positively, which played out in my actions and how I approached or handled life lessons. I've since forgiven everyone that have hurt me and weren't able to see my worth, because that has no bearing on the value I place on myself. My life has always been about showing and proving and today I'm no longer interested in showing or proving anything to anyone. Everything that I've been through has been transmuted into my purpose it was necessary for me to grow through what I went through in order for me to help those in need.

For a long time I had no clue what my purpose was I felt I was being pulled in so many directions, it wasn't until I got quiet and asked God to reveal my purpose to me that's when things began to take shape. People were leaving my life without arguments or fights. It was a purging that God was doing in order to push me into my purpose. I now understand my purpose is to help others by inspiring, motivating, and transforming lives. I've always been selfless in helping those in need and knowing what I'm called to do makes it so much easier to wake up every morning knowing that my job is to inspire others to be their best selves. Keep in mind I'm still a work in progress and have days where I have to ask God for forgiveness for doing something not pleasing in his eyes. My goal at this point is to become an inspirational/motivational/transformational speaker where I share my story to help inspire and transform lives. I want to become the light that people are seeking. I'm not here to be average by any means necessary I'm hear to stretch the limits off my destiny and transform my life in order to transform someone else's life

We go through situations to gain insight and clarity as to how to navigate through life, next time a situation arises welcome it, learn from it, and grow through it. I understand now, that my purpose is tied to my pain and that's why it's important that I help those in need overcome their obstacle and find their purpose in life. If you've gained any insight from reading my story please know that you can and will overcome anything meant to disrupt your life, it's proven that your life improves by transforming your mindset. I had to transform my mindset to see the necessary changes I wanted to see in my life. I've lost friends, businesses, loved ones, family members, and relationships and I never picked up a drink or drug. I had to change my mindset to rely on something else other than drugs.

The changes in my life began when I stopped using drugs and started focusing on bettering myself. I knew that if I didn't stop using I would end up dead. I had already been in rehabs, jails, and death would be the outcome if I continued to self medicate. I wanted a better life and envisioned myself living a better life in spite of my external environment and the lies that I told myself for majority of my life. The vision I had for my life is what I clung to in addition to having faith and doing the work. My first task was to stay clean, if I could stay clean I could show up as a willing participant in my life so I focused on 90 meetings in 90 days doing the work and cleaning up the wreckage of my past. Was it easy? Absolutely not. There were days I wanted to quit but I knew that I would be doing myself a disservice if I did that. So I just prayed and weathered every life lesson that came my way. Once I became strong in my recovery and the obsession and compulsion to use was lifted. I felt I could now begin to devise a plan of action over my life.

That plan of action included how I would approach obstacles when they presented themselves. I had no reservations to use drugs no matter what I went through or would go through. My approach to how I handled things is what changed my mindset, the reason I say that is because I had already seen how God was blessing and transforming my life so it was hard for me to come to trust and believe in him and still have doubts. Through my Spiritual Program I met God, I came to believe in a power greater than myself and I chose that power to be God. What this allowed me to do was become more God reliant instead of self reliant. I saw God in everything I was doing even when I was acting out. Seeing God in everything I did gave me a sense of gratitude. I was thankful for everything and that began to shape my thinking. I learned to show up and do the work and leave the results up to God. In return my life was impacted positively.

In coming to know God I made a decision to turn my will and life over to the care of God as I understood him to be, that allowed me to get out the way of self sabotaging with my thinking. This taught me patience, which I am still working on as we speak. This taught me a great deal about myself. What I'm learning is that patience is a skillset that I wasn't willing to learn for a long time. Almost everything that produces patience is a situation that we would rather not go through. The bible states in James 1:2-3 "my brethren, count it all joy when you fall into various trials, knowing that the testing of your faith produces patience. Here we see that the testing of our faith produces patience. Here I was working on my faith but lacked patience. The two didn't go hand in hand. I had to turn my will and life over to the care of God and ask him for help in this area.

So many times I turned my will over to God and quickly took it back because I felt God was taking too long to handle the situation. This tug of war never ended in my favor because when I did things on my own account it was done prematurely and not with good faith or intent, so I would have to tuck my tail and ask god for forgiveness and do it the right way. When I began to trust God in all things my patience started to build along with my faith. In all that I have been through my relationship with God is very important to me because in him I see me.

As I said earlier the biggest test that I'm working on is my patience. I do believe that patience is attainable and although its not one of my strongest suit. I'm willing to learn the skillset in order to succeed in this area. One of the ways I'm learning patience is with myself. For years I had no patience with myself. I've always been critical and hard on myself pushing myself and today I give myself permission to mess up and learn from the mistakes I make. I give myself permission to laugh through my pain and not take myself seriously. I'm learning to love all of me including my imperfections. I affirm who I am everyday. I tell myself that I am beautiful, worthy, deserving, and ready for all that the universe has in store for me. On days where I feel inadequate I help others. This helps me to get out of my feelings and help those in need. The reward I get from helping others can never be measured to any drugs I ingested. Helping people is what I'm most passionate about. I love the woman I am today. I am thankful that I'm able to share my testimony with others and inspire those who I come into contact with. These are the things that mean the most to me. I could never find those things in drugs or material possessions.

I spend time sharing my experience, strength, and hope with others to inspire and invoke a change in them. I currently do speaking engagements with women in different treatment facilities. My goal is to build a brand around helping others find their purpose starting with my own non-profit that I'm currently working on. In an effort to build my brand I had to put my life on the line and tell my story. I wanted this book to be transparent, honest and to really speak to the issues that plague women such as low self esteem, self worth, valuation, and bad choices; I wanted this book to be an inspiration of hope and courage to those in need. My life hasn't been an easy one but it was necessary to shape, mold, and birth the woman I am today and for that I'm truly thankful to God for carrying me and blessing me abundantly.

My life has been one hurricane after another and none of them have been life threatening as they appeared to be. I weathered the storms and made it through those storms with the help of God, my family and the village of women in my life that carried me when at times I couldn't carry myself. There were times when I wanted to completely end it all, then I remembered who I am and the lineage of warrior women that I was birthed from, who despite the odds didn't give up. I've come full circle and love the woman I am today. I was purposed to grow through what I went through in order to birth the woman I longed to become. The woman I am today is strong, resilient, faithful, God fearing, inspiring, selfless, and a beautiful soul. Life is definitely what you make it and I'm here to make the rest of my life the best of my life.

CPSIA information can be obtained
at www.ICGtesting.com
Printed in the USA
BVOW03s0830310717
490701BV00001B/21/P